Defending Dakota

Gold Coast Retrievers

Elsie Davis

Sweet Romance Publishing

Sweet Romance Publishing

Sweetromancepublishing.com

PO Box 778

Liberty, NC 27298

~To Rudolph Valentino -
the golden retriever who left pawprints in the
garage and on our hearts forever~

Chapter One

♥

"Am I nuts for doing this, Halo?" Dakota scratched behind the dog's ears, knowing it was one of his favorite spots. "I know it's crazy, but surely you understand. I mean, you've been amazing, and you've helped me a lot. I don't know what I'd have done without you, but this...this is closure. It's something I need to do."

She half expected her golden retriever to answer her one of these days. And not for the first time, she wished he could. Four years ago, she'd read an article on Reel Life, the social media site dedicated to sharing life stories. It had given her hope that one day she could put the pain of the past behind her. The article had featured a story about Carol Graves, a woman who bred retrievers specifically for use as rescue, special needs, and therapy dogs. The breeder was very selective who took the puppies home and had clear rules regarding their training.

The woman lived on the outskirts of Redwood Cove, and Dakota had been quick to pay her a visit. She was grateful Carol had understood her need and approved Halo to come home with her. Luckily, Dakota's aunt and uncle had fallen in love with Halo and were completely on board with her bringing a new dog into their posh California home. As far as they were concerned, anything that brought comfort, security, and peace to Dakota was okay by them—including a seventy-pound dog.

Getting Halo four years ago was the best decision she'd ever made. Dakota was more emotionally settled than she could remember. She was respected by her peers within the gemologist society, valued by clients worldwide for her expertise in designing unique jewelry, and partner with her uncle in the Decadence Designs jewelry store he'd started with her late father. Life was good. Stable. Secure.

Until a picture in the tabloids changed everything.

Dakota gazed out the window at the flower garden, trying to push the image from her mind. Halo nudged her hand, making sure she was aware he was right there where she needed him. The dog had an uncanny ability to sense her emotions and when she needed help to regain her focus.

She inhaled and exhaled, letting out a deep breath of air. "I've made a list, and we need to go to the store for supplies." Halo barked. "Of course, you're coming. It's not like I leave you behind very often, and you know it." The two of them were practically inseparable, but sometimes business mandated she go alone. Those were the times toughest on Dakota.

She opened the passenger door of her X-terra and let Halo jump in the front seat. Dakota unbuttoned her sweater as she came around the back of the truck. As fall days went, it was unseasonably warm. The weatherman had been quite a bit off on his prediction this morning. But it was good news as far as she was concerned. Creeping around Victor Mateo's house in the dark tonight would be bad enough, cold and dark would have been miserable.

Dakota put the truck in drive and drove through Redwood Cove, headed for the five-and-dime store. She drove past the Pacific Coast Adventures office, where all the adventurous souls in town would flock early to get signed up for their favorite activities the area had to offer. The Sweets and Treats shop was quiet this time of the afternoon, making it hard to resist the temptation to stop in to get her and Halo a treat. It was the only place in town that had people and dog food on the menu.

A flurry of activity in front of the bridal shop forced her to slow down. The annual wedding-gown sale. Out in front of the store, racks and racks of wedding gowns lined the sidewalk. Women flocked to Redwood Cove, hoping to find something unique and beautiful for their special day, all at a bargain price.

Good luck.

It was like women became obsessed when they fell in love and a man put a ring on their finger. *Totally ridiculous.* Why couldn't they get married in a dress they would wear any other day of the year? It was a waste of time and money, but to each his own. And thankfully, nothing she'd ever have to deal with, at least not anytime soon.

Dakota was happy living with her aunt and uncle, and she had Halo. What else did a woman need? The few dates she'd been out on were proof she wasn't ready for anything with anyone. The reality was that no one could ever meet up to the ideal of her father or the love her parents shared. She'd seen it firsthand and had no intentions of accepting anything less from anyone.

She pulled into a parking spot in front of the store. "Here we are, boy." Opening the door, she slid out of the truck, Halo's leash in hand. He moved to sit in the driver's seat and waited for her to put on his special harness that labeled him as a therapy dog. It gave him special privileges when it came to going into businesses, and it helped keep people away from trying to pet him. He was a full-time working dog, although Dakota liked to refer to him as her best friend.

Aisle after aisle, she pushed the shopping cart and led Halo around the store, picking out what they needed for her mission tonight. Black tights. Black turtleneck. Black skin paint. Black ski mask. Black gloves. Black backpack.

"I think that's it. We need to get home and work on the rest of the details. We don't have much time left." She patted Halo's head, and he wagged his tail in agreement.

She headed toward the checkout, almost bumping carts with a man who had the same idea. "I'm sorry. You go ahead." Dakota pointed to the cashier.

The man was incredibly attractive. Brown eyes. Wavy brown hair. A five o'clock shadow that only added to his appeal. But he was apparently incapable of speech.

Dakota pointed again. "You can go first. It's fine. You don't have nearly as much as I do." She smiled at him, trying to be friendly.

He glanced at her cart, then at Halo, and then back at her. His frown spoke volumes. She'd met people like him before and didn't care what he thought of her bringing a dog into the store.

"Thanks." He nodded, turned, and dumped his three items on the conveyor belt. A bag of chips, a six pack of soda, and a chocolate bar. His dinner would be about as exciting as he was judging by the quality of food he was buying. Too much sugar. Maybe that's what ailed his personality.

He was gone minutes later, but not before he cast her one last derisive glance.

Good riddance.

Halo nudged her hand as if sensing her discomfort. She rubbed his head to let him know she was fine. It wasn't like she was going to let some jerk ruin her night. Tonight, she was going right a thirteen-year wrong.

Chapter Two

♥

SEVERAL BARKING DOGS COULD be heard in Chandler Chase, the fancy neighborhood in Redwood Cove where wealthy and famous people had moved to get out of San Francisco. The gated community offered a golf course, tennis courts, a clubhouse, and a swimming pool, but Dakota was only interested in one place. Victor Mateo's mansion.

"Halo, sit." Dakota issued the command in a low voice, knowing sound traveled in the darkness like it had wings. The dog looked from side to side, keeping close tabs on any activity around them. She reached down to stroke the silky fur on the side of his neck, drawing strength and courage from her furry friend.

Victor's house was in darkness, just as she'd suspected it would be. As much as she'd rather be anyplace else, she wasn't about to give into her fear and run away. Dakota had come too far to turn back now, and she owed it to her parents to make things right. Something she'd failed to do the night they died. She crouched low to avoid detection by any passing cars or nosy neighbors, heading for the white trellis on the side of the house.

"The coast is clear. Stay, Halo. Guard." He licked her hand in understanding, but she couldn't feel his wet tongue through her glove. "Good boy." He was great at many things, but climbing a trellis wasn't one of them.

She gave him one last pat before putting her first foot on the highest rung of the vine-covered trellis that she could reach, and then pulled herself up, testing the ability of the structure to hold her weight. Halo whimpered. "*Shhh*. It'll be okay. I'll be right back. Stay, Halo."

Dakota started to climb. It was a short climb to the second floor bedroom window she'd unlocked before leaving the last time she visited. Dakota hoped no one else had discovered what she'd done and relocked it as that would put an end to her plan.

It wasn't exactly breaking and entering if she didn't have to break in—at least to her way of thinking. Besides, she only wanted to get back what belonged to her in the first place.

Her mother's jewelry.

"We have a problem." Colt's earbud crackled to life, delivering words he didn't want to hear.

"What's up?" he asked in a low voice, not wanting the sound to carry across the darkened study where he lay in wait for Mateo.

His partner and friend, Jack Lucas was a veteran FBI agent, and there were only three reasons he would break radio silence. Stationed in front of the stucco mansion, his partner was keeping an eye out for anyone coming and going. So, either Mateo had arrived, the buyer meeting Mateo to get the stolen Wingate jewels had arrived, or they had an unwanted visitor. He hoped to heck it was Mateo, because after weeks of tailing the suspected jewel thief, he was ready to finish the job, recover the Wingate jewels, and get back to L.A. His workload wasn't getting any lighter stuck in Redwood Cove waiting for Mateo to make his move.

"What's going on?" Colt asked again when no answer came.

"Sorry. Was trying to get a better image. We picked up two moving heat sources close to the house. No sign of Mateo. I'm closing in to get a better look." A few seconds later, Jack confirmed the worst of the three options. They had an unwanted visitor.

"Where?" With any luck, it would be a couple of stray dogs or some other animals that had wandered on to the property, because otherwise, they had more trouble on their hands than planned.

"Garden side of the house. They entered at the back of the property and headed straight for the side. Hang on, I'm almost there." Jack's voice was barely a whisper, but the silence inside the house made it easy for Colt to hear. "Unsub is scaling the trellis and out of reach. Looks human sized but is crawling up the wall like a spider."

"You been watching too many cartoons. Must have Catwoman on your brain." Colt chuckled.

"Laugh now, wise guy, but the cat is all yours. Unsub just slipped inside the second window from the top left."

A bark sounded from somewhere nearby.

"And that?" Colt asked.

"That's your new friend's watchdog. I'm backing off. Wouldn't want him to alert anyone we're out here."

"Copy that. Just keep me posted if Mateo shows up. I'll let you know when I've got the subject apprehended and silenced. If Mateo shows up before then, I'll need time to get out, with or without our new friend." The last thing he needed was a confrontation with a danger-ous guard dog. Colt wasn't afraid of much, but a previous run in with a hundred-and-twenty-pound dog determined to put a chokehold on him had changed his opinion. The scar on his throat was a daily reminder.

"Ten-four."

Stealing from a thief was never a good idea, but apparently, whoever was in the house had missed a few lessons on the criminal code of conduct. And only a fool would try to steal from Mateo and expect to live to see thirty more sunsets.

Colt stayed close to the wall, making his way toward the door, careful not to bump into anything that would alert the intruder to his presence. If the perp was after the Wingate jewels, it would be easy for Colt to get the drop on him. He waited and listened for any sound that could be heard above the pounding of his heart as adrenaline rushed through his body. Gun drawn and ready to act, Colt was in his element.

The door of the study was pushed opened slowly, inches at a time. A beam of light danced across the walls as the man did a quick check of the room. It came dangerously close to where Colt stood stock-still, but luckily slid past his half-hidden location.

The man was small, relatively short, and dressed all in black. The moonglow through the window added to the effect, and Colt realized Jack was right—the man did look like a cat. It was a little early for trick or treating.

The intruder moved across the room to face the side wall, directing the flashlight beam onto the small framed photographs that hung in a group not far from where Colt had stood moments earlier. *Strange.* Mateo's safe was on the other side of the room behind his Guy Harvey painting. Even if the perp turned out to be an art thief, the massive original of the Orca whales was the true masterpiece in the room, not Mateo's personal photo collection.

The man unhooked one of the frames and set it on the floor against the wall. Shrugging off a backpack Colt hadn't noticed before in the darkness, the perp drew out an object and placed it on his head. A second beam of light flashed on from a headlamp before the flashlight was extinguished and put away in the backpack. The guy pulled a stethoscope from his bag, wrapped it around his neck, and then put the ends in his ears.

Colt got a better look when the perp shone his headlamp on the place vacated by the photo. A second safe. That was something they hadn't known.

Thanks for the information, mister, but you picked a bad night to come calling.

With the man intent on cracking the safe, Colt moved in closer. He grabbed the guy from behind, wrapping his arm around the man's throat as he shoved the barrel of his Glock into his back. "Not a word. Nod your head if you understand." Colt kept his voice low, mindful Mateo was due to arrive any minute.

The thief's head bobbed slightly, enough for Colt to receive the message.

"No sudden moves or I'll shoot. Understand?" Shooting was only an option in life-threatening situations, and Colt wasn't even sure this guy had a gun, but the order always sounded good.

Again, the head bobbed. Colt released his hold on the man's throat long enough to grab his handcuffs. "Hands behind your back where I can see them."

The perp complied all too easily. Rookie thief and out of his league. Poor guy should have stayed home tonight. Slapping a cuff on one of the man's wrists and then the other, he turned the guy around, but the bright light of the head-light was blinding.

Colt rummaged through the backpack to find the flashlight. He turned it on and flicked off the headlamp to get a better look. As his eyes adjusted to the light, his gaze met large blue eyes that pierced him with a healthy mixture of fear and daggers. The mask covered the rest of the face, except for their small mouth, but it was enough for Colt to suspect the truth.

Catwoman.

"What are you doing here? Are you out of your mind, lady?" His voice rose higher than the situation permitted, and he focused on reining back his agitation.

Perversely, she nodded and gave a shrug that didn't help him in the slightest. Her eyes never left his gun.

"You can answer my questions. Let's make this quick before the entire night is turned into a disaster." *And quite possibly the entire investigation.*

"You s-said not to talk. I don't like guns." The catch in her sweet voice matched the slight tremble of her body.

He lowered his gun, the terror in her eyes real. "I give you permission to speak. Why are you here?" Her gaze followed his gun.

"I can't t-tell you."

The woman had to be out of her mind. Someone must have put her up to this, because she was far too naïve to be here on her own. For all she knew, he could be a criminal, and yet she stood here defying him.

He holstered his gun and covered it with his shirt. "You're not the one calling the shots, and I'm running out of patience."

She lifted her gaze, took a deep breath, and exhaled. The transformation was incredible. Gone was the fear, and it's a place, a renewed strength.

"Look, mister, I don't know what you're after, but there's no reason we can't both get what we want and leave." Hands on hips, she faced off with him.

Ahhh. Now he understood her angle. And it was a good idea if they weren't after the same merchandise, otherwise, he who had the gun won. Except he wasn't there to steal anything, he was there to bust Mateo.

The Wingate jewels were worth over ten million dollars, and the FBI was almost positive Mateo had stolen them from the Embassy Palace Suites in New York City while the Duchess of Wingate was in residence a few months ago. But without the stolen jewels, they couldn't arrest him or return the precious jewels to their rightful owner, and Colt's boss wanted the case closed yesterday. The heat was raining down from all sides because it was such a prominent case—the heist a definite embarrassment to the United States.

"What is it you're after?" Colt asked.

"Something that belongs to me. To my family. I don't owe you anything else in the way of explanation. Who are you anyway?" The catch in her voice caught his attention when she mentioned her family, but there was no way he believed her. If Victor had something of hers, why wouldn't she go to the police and let them handle it instead of risking her life coming here?

"Your second-worst nightmare. Name's Colt Jackson. FBI." He pulled his bureau badge out and shined the light on it for her to see better. "And as to the explanation, I see it differently. You managed to drop smack in the middle of a stakeout. And now you're stuck with me until the night is over and we bust Mateo."

There was no way he could let her go anywhere and take a chance she would tip Mateo off if she was lying. And if she wasn't lying, he was doing her a favor by saving her from her own worst mistake.

"I can leave the same way I came. No one would be any wiser. If you take Mateo out, I can come back for my personal belongings later." Fool woman was still trying to negotiate her way out of this.

"Except it doesn't work that way. You know too much, and I'm not a trusting kind of guy." *Especially when it comes to trusting women.*

"Well, I'm not staying with you." Her voice had become defiant.

He reached out to pull her mask off, but it didn't slip off as he expected. "That's where you're wrong. You'll stay until I say you can leave. What's your name?" he asked. "And what's with the mask?"

"It's sewn to my shirt. Are you arresting me? I haven't done anything wrong. What I came for belongs to me."

There it was again. The same indignant voice rife with emotion. But it didn't change a thing.

"No, I'm not arresting you. But I could have you arrested for trespassing with criminal intent. I could also call Victor Mateo to inform him the woman we've been trailing broke into his home. And that we caught her in his office trying to open his safe."

"You wouldn't dare! He'd kill me," she snapped, taking a step back. Her eyes widened, fear evident in their depths.

"Exactly. And if I were trying to get you killed, I could save myself the trouble and take you out now. But I'm not, so make it easy on yourself and agree to sit tight with me and keep quiet until he shows up. And if you're a good girl and tell me who you are and exactly what you're after, I'll think about whether I believe you and what to do about it." He didn't think she'd warn Mateo. Her reaction to his threat had been too real. But he couldn't take the chance she'd double-cross him.

"That's not fair. I guess I should be relieved you don't want to arrest me or kill me. Makes a girl feel a little better standing here in handcuffs and in a dark room with a strange man." Heavy sarcasm laced her voice, reminding him of the two very different personalities this woman exhibited. "Besides, he's not coming home tonight, which is obviously something you and your sources didn't know. And it's exactly why I'm here tonight." Her chin rose a notch.

"What do you know about his whereabouts?" Colt asked, his patience running out. If what she said was true, they were here on a fool's errand.

"His plans changed, and he's away overnight. I accidentally overheard a conversation of his." She grinned.

"Accidentally, huh?" He didn't believe a word of it. Nothing this woman did would be an accident. She was too methodical and sure of herself.

"You can't hold me more than twenty-four hours without bringing Victor in on this. Which clearly, you don't want to do."

"You're trespassing. Reasonable suspicion."

"Says who? I've got a key to this place. You'd look pretty silly arresting me."

If what she said was true, it would look bad. *Why would she have a key and not use it?*

"Here's the deal. I'll stay with you willingly on two conditions. One, you give me five minutes alone in Victor's study after you arrest him, and you let me keep what I recover because I'll have provided you proof of ownership." She was relentless in her determination to get back whatever it was she was after. It made him more and more curious to find out what she wanted.

Keeping watch over her was completely within his authority, letting her alone at the scene of the crime for five minutes was not. He could always agree now and revoke the decision when the time came—although his word had always been a shield of honor. The problem was he liked to do things by the book and cooperating with Catwoman didn't fall under protocol. But the important thing was to keep her safe *and* keep her from blowing the investigation.

Dakota was right about only being able to hold her for twenty-four hours without charging her, which wasn't nearly long enough. She was asking him to put his career at stake, or at the very least risk a demotion if anything went wrong, but busting Mateo was the most important thing on his agenda. "You drive a hard bargain, lady. With proof, I see no reason you can't keep something that belongs to you. The five minutes alone, I'll have to think that one through." Colt was after the Wingate collection, so letting Dakota have what belonged to her wasn't a deal killer. "What's the second condition?"

"I want you to reopen an investigation into my parents' car accident, and if there's a shred of evidence pointing to the possibility it wasn't accidental, I want you to investigate Victor Mateo as a prime suspect for their murders."

"What?" Colt wasn't shocked often, but Catwoman had managed to do just that. Murder was a serious accusation, especially when the charge was against Mateo. "Do you know what you're asking? You clearly know more about the man than most, and yet here you're in his house risking your life. Why?" Now more than ever, he saw a need to keep her safe—from herself.

"Justice."

Chapter Three

♥

AND THE FAMILY JEWELS.

But Dakota wasn't about to share that little detail yet. It would give the guy more reason to distrust her and wouldn't suit the new plan formulating in her mind. She needed time to provide him with proof of ownership and to impart her theory of what happened that horrific night thirteen years ago. If she had any hope of piecing together the truth, Colt Jackson, FBI agent, was her man. He had the authority *and* the power to make a difference. Now all she needed to do was convince him to help her.

Operation Locket, as she'd dubbed her plan, had been laid out in detail. The only thing she hadn't counted on was the FBI. Three long months of planning had been blown in one not-so-magical moment, and now everything was in Agent Jackson's hands—including her.

Thankfully, he'd put his gun away, giving her a chance to regroup and do some fast thinking about what to do next. This was a twist she would have preferred to do without, but now that it had happened, she intended to make the most of it. Call it fate or bad luck, whatever it was, she now had an inroad to proving what she'd suspected from the minute she'd seen Victor's picture in the tabloids three months ago.

"We need to talk more, but not here. Let's go." His firm grip led her down the hallway toward the same bedroom window by which she'd entered the house earlier. "We'll go back the way you came to cover any tracks you may have left." Colt spoke to her as if she were a nuisance.

"I didn't leave any tracks," she said crossly, wishing she could get a good look at the guy holding her hostage. The flashlight pointed at her face had blacked out his features, and now the hallway was even darker without the benefit of any moonlight flooding in. Her eyes were somewhat accustomed to the darkness, but she still couldn't get a good look at him—other than the fact he was tall and had dark hair.

It comforted her to know Halo was waiting for her below. Colt was one of the good guys, and Dakota was certain that wherever they were headed, the agent would let her take her dog. The agent may not have counted on anyone landing smack in the middle of his stakeout, but she had saved them from hanging around all night for nothing, and for that, he owed her one.

Victor and his secret lady friend would have a long night ahead of them if the conversation she'd overheard earlier was anything to go by. A conversation she would have preferred not to hear.

"Jack, you copy all this. We're coming down. Assistance at the bottom would be great."

"My dog's down there. Don't hurt him."

"What kind of dog?" Colt's voice had gone sharp.

"A golden retriever. He's a special dog and won't go anywhere without me."

"Jack, the dog's a friendly golden. Move in."

Dakota turned her back to Colt to offer up the offending cuffs for removal.

"Just remember our deal. And of course, Jack is waiting at the bottom to make sure you remember."

Colt unlocked the metal bands of steel that bit into her wrists, leaving her to rub the area to ease the discomfort. Climbing down the trellis with ease, she was grateful the big lug behind her didn't get on it at the same time. The last thing she wanted to do was go crashing to the ground if the structure collapsed under the weight of two people.

Halo barked a couple of times.

"Can you shut the dog up. We don't need to announce our presence."

"Halo, quiet." He obeyed instantly. "Good boy."

As she neared the bottom, two hands grabbed her around the waist and hoisted her to the ground. Jack presumably.

Halo growled. "Easy boy. It's okay." She turned and patted the dog's head, using her soothing voice to let him know she was okay.

Within seconds, Dakota found herself back in handcuffs for the second time that night. "Are these really necessary?" she asked sarcastically, grateful her arms were at least in front of her this time.

"For the time being, yes. Just as a precaution." The faint odor of cigarettes clinging to his clothes explained the deep, rasp of his voice.

Colt jumped the last several feet to the ground. He glanced down at Halo and then back away. "Everything okay?"

"Right as rain," Jack answered. "Cuffed and ready to roll."

"And totally unnecessary, if I might add," Dakota said in a huff.

The men surrounded her on either side, leaving Halo to follow behind. They headed toward a van parked a little way away on the side of the street. Her own car was around the block, but for now, she had no choice but to leave it there.

If Victor saw it there could be trouble, and she considered letting the guys know, but she hated the idea of anyone else driving her car. Aside from Halo and her aunt and uncle, her parents' old Mustang was the next best thing in her life. Memories of riding in the car with them were fresh in her mind.

"How'd you get here?" Colt asked.

It was like he'd read her mind, either that, or he was one of those overly efficient people doing his job. "It's parked around the block. Out of sight," she added smugly, "which is more than I can say for where you parked."

"What kind of car?" Jack asked, ignoring her comment.

"Blue Mustang. Why?" she asked, frowning.

"I'm on it," Jack said, as if his words explained everything.

She turned to look back at Colt. "On what?" she demanded.

"He'll have your car relocated to headquarters."

"Nobody drives my car. It's safe for the night right where it's at." At least she hoped it was.

"You don't think come morning neighbors will get suspicious and call it in? Now's not the time to be uptight about your car. And besides, no one is driving it; he'll have it towed."

Jerk. It stunk he was right. "Fine."

"Glad we can agree." He shoved open the door and gave her a nudge. She crouched over and crawled into the vehicle.

The inside looked exactly as she'd seen on TV. Fully loaded with high-tech electronics and looking exactly like something the government would use. Dakota felt some of her tension ebb away, more confident these guys were exactly who they claimed to be.

Colt supported her as she plunged into one of the open captain seats in the back. Without the use of her hands, she would have toppled off to the other side without his help. Halo jumped in after her, curling up in a ball at her feet.

"Good boy," Dakota said as much for his benefit as hers. Jack climbed into the driver's seat and started the van. "We making a pit stop?" he asked, looking back at Colt through the rearview mirror for confirmation.

"Drive to the outskirts of town on Highway 17. Pull over into one of the Cliff Walk scenic lookouts. Should be relatively quiet out that way this time of night."

"Why are we going there?" she asked, self-preservation causing her tension to ramp up with the oddity of his request.

"For privacy."

"Privacy for what?" she asked nervously. The badge looked real, and Colt didn't come across as a bad guy, but what if she was wrong? What if it had all been a ruse to get her to come along without a fuss?

"Not what you're thinking. Relax. We have no intentions of hurting you. But we need to know more about you in order to figure out what to do with you until this is over." His answer made perfect sense, for the most part. But more importantly, Halo no longer seemed concerned with the strangers, and he was an excellent judge of character.

"That's good to know," she said dryly.

Dakota looked out the window and knew exactly where they were, which was comforting. Redwood Cove wasn't a big place, but the quaint village drew thousands of tourists each year who wanted to experience the coastal beauty. For Dakota it was home. Having lived here all her life, it was easy to spot various landmarks signaling how far out of town they traveled before Jack pulled over to the side of the road into the first vista overlook.

The five-mile scenic trail along the coast was like her own personal stomping grounds, a place where she and Halo visited several times a week for a walk or a jog, hoping to catch sight of the whales that passed by the area. The other days were spent at the dog park. It was a compromise that worked well for them both.

Colt flipped on the light; the brightness shattering the darkness inside the vehicle. Dakota squinted, trying to adjust her eyes to the change. She finally got a good look at the man seated next to her, but her image of an FBI agent and Colt had nothing in common. *Where were the glasses and thinning hair?*

Dark, wavy hair matched gorgeous brown eyes, making his handsome face seem almost exotic. Razor stubble lined his chin and the sides of his face, which only served to increase the intensity of his glaring eyes. *I've seen this man before.* The guy in the store. "You? You've got to be joking."

"You know me?" Colt asked.

He'd find out soon enough, so she didn't bother to answer.

"Fine. Have it your way." He pulled out a pocketknife and proceeded to cut a few threads and then pull against the seam to break the rest. He slid the black skull cap off her head, peeling it upward and taking the headlamp with it in one fell swoop. As the cap slipped free, it released the long, black tresses she'd carefully concealed.

She waited for him to recognize her from when they met at the store earlier today. Instead, both men looked at her, astonishment clearly etched on their faces. Although her hair was pretty, there was certainly nothing unique enough about it to cause their reaction.

"Are you kidding me?" Colt said in disgust.

She didn't like his tone. "What is your problem? First, you're rude at the store, and now you're acting like a jerk. Are you ever nice?"

The two men looked at each other and then back at her, a silent message passing between them with just a nod.

"Dakota Mitchell," Colt said, shaking his head from side to side.

She noticed he hadn't answered her question. "You know my name?"

"Victor Mateo's girlfriend. Of course, we know you. We have tons of photos of you coming and going on a regular basis lately from this place."

"I'm not his girlfriend," she said, sickened by the suggestion. Nothing could be further from the truth. Not only was he old enough to be her grandfather, but Dakota was almost positive he was a murderer. There was no way she wanted anyone to connect her with the devil incarnate in such a personal and intimate way. She shuddered, trying to dispel the image.

"Okay, so his squeeze bunny of the month. Is that why you're trying to steal from him? Did he end it with you, and you aren't satisfied with his parting gift?" She liked Colt's second assumption even less.

"You're disgusting. You're lucky I'm in handcuffs, because I wouldn't take such rudeness from any man without a fight." Halo was on his feet and looking back and forth between them.

"And any physical retaliation would land you in jail for assaulting an FBI agent," Colt said, his voice cold and crisp.

"Assuming you really are one. You haven't even read me my rights." She did believe them, but his attitude irritated her.

Jack threw his head back and laughed. "She's a feisty little thing."

Colt glanced at Jack with a stern expression on his face before turning back to her. "I've already explained you're not under arrest, so there are no rights to be read. Detaining you is as much for your own protection as it is for the integrity of the investigation."

But nothing happened tonight. "How is it for my protection?"

"Whatever it is you planned on taking, my guess is Victor Mateo would know the first place to go looking for it, if in fact it's something that belongs to you. Coming and going as you do gives you the means, and your claim of ownership gives you motive."

"So, does that mean you believe me?" It wasn't as if she hadn't considered Victor thinking she had something to do with the disappearance of the jewelry, but she'd covered her tracks and had a great alibi. As far as everyone else was concerned, she was out of town on a business trip—and nowhere near Redwood Cove.

"I'm withholding judgement and playing both sides. Either way, you're stuck with me." His tone brooked zero opposition, and Dakota knew she wouldn't win any extra points in trying to win him over to help her if she continued to fight him.

"Give me your hands," Colt ordered. He unlocked the cuffs, and the circulation in her arms started to return. She reached out to pat Halo on the head, scratching him behind the ear. "Thank you."

Colt nodded but didn't say a word.

"So where to, Colt? It's your call," Jack spoke up from the front seat, clearly amused.

Dakota was at a loss to understand his humor. Nothing about this situation was funny.

"My place. It will work as a safe house, and I'll keep watch over her until this is over."

"Boss won't like it," Jack answered.

"We don't have a lot of options with this short notice and for this short of time. We can't take a chance on her tipping off Mateo. If you'll handle the paperwork tonight, I'll handle her. Tell the boss we need a few more days. It's not like there's any chance of me crossing any professional lines with Victor Mateo's leftovers." Colt's desultory tone was like acid on her skin, his judging look hurting her in a way she hadn't felt in a long time.

Chapter Four

♥

NOTHING COULD HAVE PREPARED Colt for the identity of the woman staring at him with wide eyes and a pixie face when he removed the hood covering her head. It was a face he knew all too well, having seen it over and over the past few weeks during the stakeout and then again today at the store.

Watching her come and go from Mateo's home on a regular basis, Colt knew almost everything there was to know about her. Up close, she was more stunning than the photos did her justice. Of course, the black skin-tight leotard that revealed every inch of her curvy body didn't hurt the image. She could command the attention of any man, which left only one reason someone looking like her would hang out with the likes of Mateo. *Money.*

It was a tragedy to see her wasted on the scumbag. Always impeccably attired, high heels accenting her long, slender legs, she was a walking dream. The pictures never showed her smiling, something he'd picked up on almost immediately. Hour after hour with nothing to do but watch Mateo's place had left Colt wondering about her story. About what could have possibly happened to create the sad, faraway look he saw in her eyes. The photographs didn't lie.

If she was unhappy there, why did she bother to go? *"I want to prove Victor murdered my parents."* Her words echoed in his head. Was it possible she could be telling the truth?

The report he'd read on her stated she lived with her aunt and uncle and had since she was twelve, after both parents died in a car accident. Her parents had been wealthy, well-respected members of the community. Dakota had gone to Redwood College for her associate degree in business and then on to earn a degree from the

Gemological Institute of America. Currently, she specialized in appraising jewelry and acted as the buyer for Decadence, the Mitchell's family custom jewelry retailer here in town. Having grown up in the business, it was no wonder she had accomplished by the age of twenty-five what others could only hope to accomplish by the time they were in their mid-thirties.

She was a successful gemologist, working in a lucrative business, and hanging out with Mateo. A jewel thief. Something was very wrong with the picture, and it was his job to make sure nothing stood in the way of him arresting Mateo and recovering the stolen Wingate jewels. Including Dakota Mitchell.

Seeing her every day with Victor had irritated him. He'd become almost unnaturally possessive toward the woman, and he didn't even know her, or like her, for that matter. But his fascination had only grown deeper, and he'd found himself continually wondering what she was like in person. The dark-haired beauty deserved more than the likes of Mateo, but there was nothing he could do about it—professionally or personally.

She was playing with fire by double-crossing Mateo. Taking her to his house might not be the smartest thing to do under the circumstances, but it would allow him to keep an eye on her and keep her safe. It had nothing to do with the woman, or nothing he was willing to admit to anyway. His comment to her had been rude, and he'd known instantly from her pained expression that he'd hit below the belt, but there was nothing he could do about it now.

At least not under the watchful eyes and ears of his partner. Maybe later, when this was over, he'd explain. And apologize. Colt knew he was treading a fine line. He was known for following protocol to a T, and any deviation from the norm would alert Jack and it wouldn't take long for his partner to put his finger on the truth. Not that his partner would out him, but if the bureau got wind, then there would be trouble.

Jack drove in silence to Colt's place, but his frequent glances in the rearview mirror relayed his unspoken thoughts. Colt was the lead on the case, and the decision regarding Dakota was his call. Under normal circumstances, he would take Jack's opinion under serious consideration. His objection was probably based on the assumption Colt was attracted to Dakota. That might be true, but this was purely business, and something he was quite qualified to handle.

Colt turned his attention back to Dakota. She sat stiffly in her seat, her body pressed against the side wall of the vehicle, one hand on Halo's back.

"What is it you think Mateo has of yours?" he asked, trying to get to the bottom of her accusations and her claim.

"Do you promise to give me five minutes in his office after you arrest him?" The hope in her voice was unmistakable.

Colt shrugged. "I said I'd think about it. You still need to prove to me what you want to take is yours, and you need to convince me why you think Mateo has it. I suggest you start trying, especially based on your second condition. Murder is a serious charge, and I need to understand why you think he murdered your parents."

"What do you know about me? I presume you've run a search since you know my name."

"I have. I know quite a bit. Name, address, education, occupation, marital status, and I've read about your parents' car accident when you were twelve. So why don't you start by telling me what you were after?" Whatever it was had to be of importance if she was willing to go to these lengths to get it back.

She cast a nervous glance first at Jack and then back at him.

"How do I know I can trust you?" The catch in her voice was a good sign she wasn't as brave as she let on. Even Halo sensed her discomfort and moved to put his head in her lap.

"I don't think you're in a position not to trust. I promise I'm one of the good guys, and I'll keep you safe from Mateo if that's what I need to do."

"But you don't believe me." It was a statement born of fact, but there was nothing he could do to dispel the notion.

"I don't need to believe you in order to protect you. Even if it's from yourself."

Jack pulled up in front of Colt's house. "You sure about this?"

His friend since the academy and his partner since he joined the jewelry theft division of the FBI five years ago, Jack knew him well. Of course, Colt's comments about Dakota the past few weeks might have tipped him off, setting off a string of endless teasing from the man. But there was no teasing in his voice now.

"It'll be fine," Colt said, trying to reassure him. Just because Dakota was gorgeous didn't mean he'd act on his interest. All he wanted was information from Mateo's most recent girl. The same girl Victor had been seeing when he stole the Wingate jewels last month. She might have valuable information, and it was his job to dig for leads. Bringing her in to interrogate her and then letting her leave ran the risk she'd run straight to Mateo and blow the investigation. It was a risk he couldn't take.

"Let's go." He reached for Dakota's hand and helped her out of the van, Halo following right behind her. Colt poked his head back inside the vehicle. "You headed back to the Redwood Cove Inn?"

"Yeah. I need to listen in to our surveillance audio to see if we can figure out what Mateo's up to."

"He's got to move the collection soon. Only a fool would hang on to them for too long. He's a jewel thief, not a collector."

"True. And, Colt, be careful."

"No worries. I'll keep you posted." Colt slid the van door closed and stepped back.

"This is your place?" Dakota asked.

"It is."

"Not what I'd have pictured for a hot-shot FBI agent. Downright normal, cookie-cutter suburbia home that looks like every other home on the street. Why is that?"

He looked at the house lit up with security lights and didn't like it a whole lot either, but it was his temporarily, and for now, it was Dakota's safe house. "Glad you like it," he said, unable to keep the sarcasm from his voice. "It's just a place to sleep and eat. A person doesn't need anything more."

"What about family? Wife? Girlfriend? A home is more than what you describe."

He led her up the sidewalk, Halo sticking close by, sniffing each bush they passed.

This wasn't supposed to get personal, so Colt avoided the answer about other people in his life. He wasn't celibate by any means, but after his wreck of a mother managed to sour him on relationships, he didn't need to set up a place to attract women. Add that to the fact he was in a dangerous job, the last thing he wanted to do was put a woman in danger because of his choices.

Time to change the subject. "What about you? Why are you still living with your aunt and uncle? You're twenty-five years old, if I remember correctly. Bit old to be living in the pockets of your family, don't you think?"

"Touché. And, yes, probably. But for now, it's okay. They love me, and it makes sense based on work. Family business and all."

They stepped inside, and Colt flipped on the light. "Well, at least the cookie-cutter home, as you call it, is temporarily mine, and I can do what I want and when I want." Until this case was closed, but that was beside the point.

Although his home in L.A. wasn't much different than this. He was never there long enough to want to make it different. His job moved him around a lot, and he didn't believe in relationships, so why did he need a home? A roof over his head had been enough for as long as he could remember.

"Not much different inside." Dakota's gaze looked around the room. Through her eyes, he noticed how barren it was. "Do you actually live here, or is this just a stopover? No pictures. No art on the wall. No personal effects. What gives?"

"No time." He shrugged. "Case after case, and I don't always have the luxury of coming home every night."

"No luxury here, trust me." She smiled, but her sarcasm wasn't lost on him. She ran her long fingers ran across the back of the upholstered sofa and turned to face him. "Hope you don't mind Halo being here?"

"No. He's fine."

"So where are we sleeping tonight?"

Her question took him by surprise, and he stood there gaping like a fool.

"I meant Halo and me. Don't go getting any ideas, mister." Dakota laughed and shook her head.

"I knew what you meant," he lied.

"Yeah, right." Halo had moved to sit beside her. Those two were tight, inseparable almost.

"You can sleep in my room, and I'll sleep on the couch." He hadn't thought the sleeping arrangements through very well. The idea of Dakota in his bed was like a punch to the gut.

"As long as you don't accidentally find your way back to your own bed, I guess it will work," she teased.

"Pretty sure you're safe with me. I never get involved with suspects, clients, or anyone in between when it comes to work. Can I get you a glass of wine? I have both." It was his turn to tease her.

"Both, as in red and white?" Dakota looked somewhat confused; her brow drawn tight.

"Both, as in wine and glasses." He chuckled. He didn't have much, but he did have what he needed. "I've got a local red from Dorma Valley Winery. Good stuff, if you like wine."

"I do. Thanks. Do you have something I could change into while you're getting it. I feel a little out of place dressed like this." She scrunched up her nose as she looked down at her outfit.

He kind of like the outfit, but it wouldn't do to tell her that. "Hang on, I'll see what I can find."

Colt poured her a glass of wine before making his way down the hall to his bedroom. He crossed the room to the dresser to search the drawers for the smallest T-shirt he had, and a pair of sweatpants fitted with an elastic band and tie to help hold them up. Loose, unattractive, and therefore perfect.

He rejoined her in the living room. "Here you go. My bedroom is the first one on the left." Colt handed her the clothes.

"Thanks. Be right back." Unable to stop himself, he watched her walk away.

Five minutes later, Colt realized it didn't matter if she wore a bag, the woman was a knockout.

"Not my normal style, but I guess it will have to do. But since there's no chance of you wanting Victor's leftovers, it's not like I have to dress to impress." Colt choked on the barbed comment delivered with a smile. He deserved it, but it didn't make it any easier to accept.

"I'm sorry. I shouldn't have said that earlier. At least not in your presence." By way of apology, it was lame, but it was the best she'd get out of him.

"You shouldn't have said it at all. You're judging something you know nothing about, and for the last time, you're wrong." She sounded sincere. And more than anything, Colt wanted it to be the truth.

"Okay then, tell me your story. Make me a believer."

She watched him carefully for a few seconds, as if trying to make up her mind. For her sake, Colt hoped she was a straight shooter. Anything less could be big problem—for them both.

Chapter Five

♥

"VICTOR STOLE MY MOTHER'S jewelry collection the night my parents died, and I think he murdered them in order to get away with it." It was the first time Dakota had ever voiced the words out loud, but she left off one piece of critical information.

Afraid no one would believe her without more proof than an awakened memory, she'd concocted her own plan, hoping to prove her theory before going to the authorities. Her inability to remember the details of the man's tattoo that night in her father's study had led to Victor getting away with grand larceny and very possibly murder. For thirteen years, she'd felt responsible the thief was never arrested. And for almost as many years, she'd connected her parents' deaths with the robbery. Once the idea took hold, it wouldn't let go. To her way of thinking, there was no way the two events were simply coincidence.

Victor Mateo had been a friend of her parents, and Dakota had used that friendship to gain access to his inner circle. His house. Suffering the man's repulsive presence, she'd tried to learn everything about him, to find something—anything that would tie him to the crimes.

The day she walked in his office and discovered him gazing at her mother's locket was the day her plan shifted from search and discover to steal back and destroy.

Colt watched her closely, but she was ready for his questions.

"Let's start with the jewelry. What makes you think he stole them? Aside from the fact he's a known jewel thief, because that's not enough evidence." Could she trust him with the truth? Or would he laugh and dismiss her memory?

It would have been easier if she could have gotten the locket first, but things hadn't worked out according to plan. She had to tell someone. Who better than an FBI agent bent on arresting Victor anyway? After losing her parents that night, she had nothing more to lose and everything to gain. Dakota took a deep breath and then exhaled.

Halo sensed her change in mood and came to sit at her feet. "Good boy." She reached for him, trying to draw strength to see this through to the end.

"I saw him," she answered deadpan.

Colt choked on his wine. "I think I'm going to need something stronger than wine for this story." He stood and headed toward the kitchen.

"I wouldn't mind something a little stronger myself for the occasion, if you don't mind." Liquid courage.

Colt turned back, his left eyebrow lifted in disbelief, but without a word, he went through the kitchen door. He came back moments later and handed her a glass, the amber liquid barely filling the glass an inch as compared to his own half glass.

She took a sip and coughed. The liquid burned her throat, causing her eyes to water. A warming sensation flooded her body, and she found herself relaxing. It was time to tell Colt what she knew. Hopefully, it wasn't too late. Because tonight, she hoped to open the final chapter in the destruction of Victor Mateo.

Colt sat down in the big armchair, his eyes never leaving her. He pulled out his phone, pressed a button and placed it on the small table between them. "For the record." He nodded toward the device. "Now start from the beginning and don't leave anything out."

She didn't care if he recorded the conversation. In fact, the less she had to retell everything later, the better. The memories were still painful and reliving that night and opening the wounds she'd tried for years to close was hazardous to her mental state. Halo nudged her hand.

Dakota set the drink down, preferring Halo for the support she needed. He laid his head in her lap and looked up at her with huge brown eyes. She tried to lose herself in their warmth, trying to separate her thoughts and feelings.

"Thirteen years ago, I was in my father's study when Victor Mateo showed up. My parents had gone out for the evening, and I'd left the book I was reading in my father's study. I'm not allowed in there without him, so I snuck in and hoped he wouldn't realize I had disobeyed him the next morning. When I was there, I heard a noise and hid behind the blue damask drapes that covered the windows."

She paused as the memories flooded her brain. Halo nudged her hand, and she continued to stroke his neck and scratch behind his ears. "The man had a gun. I could see the moonlight reflecting off it. It was huge and threatening. Enough to keep me rooted to the spot, terrified of making a sound. He was dressed all in black. After he left, I was too afraid to leave the study. When my aunt and uncle were notified that my parents had died in a car crash, they came to the house and found me in the study. I told them what happened, and the police came, but it was impossible to give the police any useful information."

Colt's gaze burned into her. She sat back against the couch, hoping to get a read on his reaction for the next part.

"Then why do you believe it was Victor Mateo? Why now, after all these years do you suddenly know his identity?"

"Because he took his jacket off and placed it on the back of my father's leather chair before he removed the painting off the wall behind the desk. When he raised his arms, the moonlight cast a clear picture of a large tattoo on the man's bicep just below the edge of his turned-up T-shirt sleeve. It looked like a red heart with a dark object piercing through the heart. Like a dagger."

Colt shrugged, giving lie to the sudden intensity in his eyes. "Not necessarily an uncommon tattoo."

"Maybe. But this one had a big snake head facing it, and the snake's body running down the entire length of his arm." A chill sliced through her as the memory came alive. Halo licked her hand and whimpered. She tried to refocus and give Halo the attention he demanded.

"I would think information like that would have been enough to put Mateo at the top of the suspect list, so what happened?" She couldn't tell if he was asking because he still didn't believe her, or if he was in interrogation mode, but he was tense.

"I don't know." His scrutiny made her uncomfortable.

"What do you mean?"

"I couldn't tell the police about the tattoo. Not then, anyway." Her fingers tapped wildly against Halo's shoulder.

"Why not?" Colt fired off the million-dollar question. She could sense his frustration.

"Not that I wouldn't. I couldn't. There's a difference."

"I'm listening." He'd leaned forward in his seat, his interest piqued.

"After Victor left, I was frozen with fear behind the curtain, afraid to move. I was only twelve. I waited all night for any sound of my parents to come home. They never came. It wasn't until morning that I heard my aunt and uncle calling my name. I was sure to be in trouble for being in the study, but I didn't care. I just wanted someone to make me feel safe. When I saw their faces, I knew something was desperately wrong. That's when they told me about my parents.

"The doctors call it selective amnesia. The fear, compounded by the grief was a double whammy, and I couldn't remember anything about the man, the tattoo, or the gun. The more they pressed for information, the further it seemed to slip away from me." She pressed her hands to her forehead to fight back the headache threatening to ensue. Over and over, the police had pressured her for answers she couldn't give.

"I'm so sorry, Dakota." Colt moved to sit next to her, taking her hand in his. His strength and warmth seeped into her soul. "What's happened since then? You obviously remember something, which means you had a trigger point. Tell me about it." It sounded like he believed her. And like he knew something about selective amnesia. It was a good start.

"I was in San Francisco for a gemologist convention and happened to see a tabloid in the hotel lobby. On the front page there was a picture of Victor and Evelyn Madding. Apparently, he was dating her at the time." She shuddered as she thought of the photograph that had unleashed a torrent of memories locked away.

"The Evelyn Madding? Three-time Oscar winning actress and the biggest sensation since Julia Roberts?"

"The one and only. Victor never goes anywhere unless he's dressed in a suit and tie. It's an image thing. Except this time, he'd taken Evelyn out on a yacht in San Francisco Bay. What should have been a private affair no one cared about became big news because it was Evelyn Madding. Paparazzi follow her like hounds after a cornered fox, and they managed to photograph the couple on the yacht. He was dressed in swim trunks, his arms wrapped around Evelyn. The tattoo on his right arm was clearly pictured.

"The image tripped something inside me, and all the memories came rushing back. This time, I could see the tattoo. The tattoo I saw that night belongs to Victor Mateo." She watched him intently for any sign he believed her. Without his support, she had nothing, and Victor would never be brought to justice.

"What if the tattoo in the photograph is what your memory latched on to in order to fill in the blanks. Like superimposing the image." The voice of reason wasn't what she wanted to hear. Of course, he didn't believe her—it was why she wanted proof first.

"Victor used to come to the house and was always at the parties my parents threw for friends. I used to hide on the stairs to watch, and

I never liked the way he watched my mother. I know he stole the jewels, and I think he killed my parents." She sat back in her seat, frustrated with the way the talk was going. Halo nudged her again, reminding her he was there.

"Okay, so let's say you're right about who stole the jewels. Why do you think he murdered them? They weren't home, so it wasn't like they were in his way, stopping him from doing the job."

Colt was still listening and still asking questions. Hope blossomed, although there wasn't much else to tell. Just a few random facts and a gut feeling.

"I don't know. The timing, I guess. The fact I think he's a snake. It's just a feeling, and I can't explain it. That's why I want both cases reopened. Particularly the accident. My mom was supposed to be at the theater with her best friend, Julia. Tickets they got courtesy of Victor, by the way. Coincidence or contrived?"

"What was your dad doing that night?" Colt asked. He'd gone into detective mode, thinking through the information and asking good questions. She'd been right to tell him.

"He always played cards on Friday nights at the club just outside of town. My parents weren't even supposed to be together when it happened. Julia told me one time, that my mom felt sick and called my father to pick her up during intermission. They were on their way home when it happened." Thirteen years later, Dakota still couldn't stop the tears from falling.

She pulled her hand away from Colt to wetness from her cheeks, hating the weakness.

"I'm sorry, but there's not much more to your story than a burglary. Do you know for a fact the jewels are in Victor's possession? Most thieves wouldn't keep the loot around for very long."

It was infuriating that no one would even consider the two events related. Granted, the only link was coincidence, but wasn't coincidence one of the big reasons law enforcement agencies solved cases. Coincidences gave direction for an investigation, something that never happened with her parent's car crash. It had been ruled accidental and the case closed.

"A week ago, I walked in on him in his study and saw him standing in front of his safe. He was holding up my mother's favorite locket, gazing at it with a strange expression on his face. She wasn't wearing it the night she died because she was dressed for the theater instead. Victor's face turned red with rage when he saw me watching, and he started shouting, ordering me to leave. He accused me of being just like my father. I think he's afraid I might have recognized the necklace. Something in his expression told me I wouldn't be invited back, so I stopped long enough to unlatch a window. There was no way I wasn't coming back for my mother's necklace. That's why you found me sneaking into his place to get what was mine instead of trying to figure out another way of recovering the jewelry that belongs to my family. The jewelry he stole." The crazed look on Victor's face had scared Dakota, and she'd left quickly, not trusting him or what he might do if he suspected the real reason she'd been visiting him the past few months.

Colt brushed his hands through his hair, deep in thought. "It doesn't make any sense why he would keep the stolen merchandise." He shook his head.

"I know what I saw, and I know I want to see if the rest of the jewelry is stashed in there with the locket." Dakota stood and crossed to the front window to gaze out, Halo following closely by her side. She needed Colt's help. Somehow, she had to convince him.

She turned back to face him, his gaze piercing her with intensity. Colt leaned forward and pressed a button on the phone. He sat back in his chair, hands clasped, pointer fingers raised like a teepee and tapping his mouth. Deep in thought, she kept silent, waiting for his decision.

"Okay." Colt drew a deep breath and then exhaled. "Off the record, I'll give you the five minutes you want. It's against my better judgment and completely against protocol, but I believe you about the jewelry."

Thank goodness. A rush of excitement filled Dakota. He was going to help. Finally, she had someone on her side. She wasn't sure what had changed his mind, but it didn't matter. The FBI would get Victor, and hopefully, she'd recover her mother's jewelry. As for the rest, well, she'd play it one step at a time. "Thank you so much."

"Well, before you get too excited, you need to understand my condition. You'll be wearing a monitor bracelet to keep you from getting any ideas of running and to keep this on the up and up as much as possible. I'm going to look over the theft report to see what was stolen, and I'm going to want to see what you're taking out to make sure they match. I'm sure the descriptions are clear and will give me what I need to know." Colt was still being the overbearing detective, but she had to play by his rules, whether she liked them or not.

"Is the monitor really necessary? I'm not going anywhere."

"It is if you want in his office."

"Fine. What about reopening the two cases?" She would agree to anything, especially if it meant Victor would pay for his crimes.

"*If* Victor is in possession of stolen property, he'll be charged as such. I'm not sure how much weight a sudden memory recollection will carry thirteen years later. As to a connection between the two events, honestly, I have nothing to go on, Dakota. I need a reason. I'm sure there was nothing out of the ordinary or it would have been investigated thoroughly. But *I will* reread both case reports if it makes you happy." He downed the last of whiskey and stood.

"Thank you. That's all I'm asking for. Someone to look them both over with a fresh set of eyes. Knowing who broke in and stole the jewelry, and that he was a friend of the family, could give things a whole new perspective."

She couldn't believe it. Colt was going to re-open the cases. Well, reread them anyway. Now all she could do was hope it would lead to more.

"What's the jewelry worth?" Colt asked.

"I don't know. I was twelve. I would expect a lot since our family is in the gem business, but I would have to see it to assess it accurately. Why do you ask?" Dakota had never thought of the monetary value, only the personal value.

"It bothers me that he kept the jewelry all this time. Or at least, the locket," Colt said, his eyebrows furrowed.

Doubt. That's all it took. One seed to water and feed and give light to make it grow. Things were looking up, and Colt might yet turn out to be her knight in shining armor. The thought made her smile.

She crossed the room to where he stood, went up on tippy toe, and planted a kiss on his cheek. "Thank you."

"I haven't done anything yet," he said, placing his hands on her arms and putting distance between them. But not before she saw the look in his eyes.

Colt Jackson was interested in her, not just her agent keeper. It was a thought she tucked away, one to consider later, when she was alone. And after this mess was over.

"But you will. I trust you will," she insisted.

"Blind trust can be heartbreaking." He was still watching her with an intensity that made her shiver. Not with fear, but with excitement.

"You're a nice guy, Colt Jackson. Don't try to shade the truth. Good night."

She made her way down the hall, Halo happily by her side. Dakota didn't dare look back at Colt. Mr. FBI, tall, dark, and irritating, was sexy as all get-out. But also, a man on the move. Which was exactly why she found herself practically running down the hall to the safety of the room he'd designated as hers until this fiasco was over.

He wasn't a man capable of the love she was looking for, and it was better to steer clear of any hero notions she might get because he was helping her.

Chapter Six

♥

IF DAKOTA WAS TELLING the truth, and Colt sensed she was, she'd been through a horrible ordeal. It was no wonder she wanted answers. His heart ached for her when he thought of her trapped with a strange man brandishing a gun. Stress-induced amnesia brought on after learning about her parent deaths was not a stretch, not by any means. He'd seen enough cases of amnesia to know how confusing and helpless a person could become when the brain went into protection mode and shut down certain traumatic memories. Most cases resolved themselves within months or even years, but in some cases, the memory was never restored.

It stood to reason a photograph could trip her memory, opening the floodgates to a past that might have been better to remain on lockdown. She was either a master at the game of deception, or she was a victim seeking justice, and Colt was putting his bets on the vindication card.

And if that part of her story was true, it left the part about her relationship with Mateo in question. He'd been so sure she was just another woman willing to toss her morals into the trash for the likes of a high roller like Mateo, willing to become his plaything. Her indignation had been genuine, and the lame apology he'd given not enough, but it would have to do—at least until he had proof.

His attraction had to remain in the no-go zone anyway. Mateo's case stood between them, not to mention he didn't live here. Didn't really have a place he called home for as much as he moved around. It had been easy to ignore the attraction when he thought of her as Mateo's playmate, but Dakota's story and her kiss had changed everything. Now he'd have to keep his distance, something made more difficult since she was living under his roof.

Thankfully, she'd retired for the night. Out of sight, but not out of mind—Colt forced himself to focus on the computer. He accessed the RCPD files, searching for information on the burglary report. Colt hadn't wanted to give Dakota false hope and tell her he would reopen the case, but he had every intention of checking out the files. He'd be laughed out of the bureau for making a wild claim of murder without a shred of evidence, which is why he would keep it to himself until he had more substantial grounds than selective amnesia reversal.

But she was right—at times, coincidence did come in handy to help solve crimes. The new information she'd presented was a strong enough reason to warrant a further look, and it was also the reason he'd promised her the five minutes she'd requested. He could get into a lot of trouble if it was discovered, but after all these years, it was the least he could do to give her back a piece of her life. And he'd never forgive himself if something went wrong and Mateo got spooked and fenced her mother's jewelry and then it was gone forever.

Hour after hour, he searched for answers and jotted down questions that came to mind. There was one big loophole in Dakota's story. There was no mention of the tattoo she claimed to have seen. She said she couldn't remember what it looked like, but that wouldn't preclude the mention of it in the police report. But under the description of perpetrator, it stated "no distinguishing marks".

An internet search turned up the photograph of Mateo and Madding, right down to the tattoo on his arm. It was exactly as Dakota described. Although, on closer inspection, Colt saw the snake's mouth was open and poised as if to swallow the heart. A sick and twisted image that told of a dark story.

He glanced at his watch. Two a.m.

Colt needed to catch some shut eye, but he simply didn't have anything new to tell Dakota.

He pulled up personal information on Mateo and his business holdings, and then searched out each of Dakota's parents and read whatever he could find, whether personal or about their jewelry store, Decadence. He wrote down important dates and places.

Looking back over his notes, his gaze caught and held on two pieces of information that linked all three people. Gold Coast Elementary and Redwood Cove High School.

Victor Mateo, Chloe Sanders, and John Mitchell had all gone to high school together and graduated the same year. Dakota had referred to Victor as a family friend, but according to some of the pictures posted from past classes on the school's website, Victor and Chloe had a history. King and queen history on prom night. They'd obviously been a very popular couple.

And yet a year later, Chloe had married John Mitchell.

Dakota said Victor used to watch her mother in a creepy way. A description he discounted at first because it was told as something witnessed through a twelve-year-old girl's eyes. Maybe he'd been too quick to dismiss the information.

It was a motive. But if Victor was in love with Chloe, why kill her? And there was still nothing to tie in the car crash. He glanced back down at his notes, willing them to point him in the right direction. He shut off the computer and turned out the lights, hoping to get some sleep. He didn't have much to tell Dakota when she woke, but it wasn't for the lack of trying.

Victor gave her opera tickets. She wasn't even supposed to be with him that night. She got sick. Dakota's words tumbled into his head.

Colt bolted upright, adrenaline rushing through his veins. It was still only a theory, but it was a theory with a little meat to it. There wasn't any evidence and no charges could be filed unless he found something. The first place to look was the accident report filed the night Dakota's parents died.

It took a little more effort to weave through the website and gain access to the Vehicle

Records Division, but he had enough motive to justify his actions. He wasn't snooping. He was investigating. And by the time he read the report, it would be too late for them to raise cane about his methods for accessing it.

Colt's attention was immediately drawn to some odd inconsistencies. Great detail was given about the occupants of the vehicle and very little about the accident itself. Officers typically wrote their reports the same way, either long descriptions or short and to the point. It was a matter of personal style, as long as they got the information down. But on this particular report, the combination of overly descriptive in some areas and short in others was an oddity.

And there was nothing to indicate Mr. Mitchell's actual blood level, only that alcohol might have been a factor. The car was never inspected, and the incident was ruled an accident as the result of drinking and driving. Case closed. Just like Dakota stated.

But it was the little details missing that bothered Colt. It could easily be laziness, but the inconsistencies caused him to consider another possibility—behind-the-scenes dirty dealing. Not to mention the coincidence of both cases happening the same night. No one had ever mentioned the other case; side note or otherwise.

Colt fired off a few emails to some of his trusted contacts and only just managed to close the computer before Dakota walked in the living room, Halo at her side.

In the early morning light, she was beautiful. Her half smile twisted his heart. The only time he'd ever seen her smile was around him. It left him filled with a deep satisfaction knowing he was at least partly responsible.

"Good morning." Colt stood. He'd pay for the lack of sleep later but couldn't help being energized when she walked in the room. This attraction he had for her was dangerous, but he trusted he could keep it under wraps. He was a professional. Halo came and sat next to him, nudging his head as if to say hello. Or maybe he was looking for food.

"Good morning," Dakota answered. "Can I have some coffee?"

"Of course. Sit down, and I'll get it for you."

He went into the kitchen and fixed two cups of instant, bold brew. He'd need a few more cups for his brain to start functioning clearly, but this would give him the initial jolt to fire it up.

He went back to the living room and handed her a cup. "Careful, it's hot. Sorry, but I don't have cream. I do have sugar though." He held out a couple of the white packets he'd collected from too many nights of hotel living.

"No, thanks. I don't use either. At work, it's too hard to mess with the fixings, and I got used to the butchering harsh reality of strong, put-hair-on-your-chest coffee."

"I'll take your word for it." Colt chuckled, trying not to think about her chest. A chest he sincerely doubted could claim even one hair. "Mine's not that strong. In fact, I think I make a good cup of coffee."

"No over-blown sense of confidence in you." Laughter looked good on Dakota.

"Nope. Just load the cup and press the button. Comes out perfect every time."

She shook her head and grinned. "It is good. But now I know your secret, and I hate to break it you, but I think half the country knows it too. I'm surprised you don't just pop into the Dessert First Bakery or the Sweets and Treats downtown to get your coffee and morning donuts. That's where most of our local law enforcement show up at some point in the morning."

"I'm trying to keep my figure, and donuts every morning would make it difficult. We do, however, need to get Halo some food. Dogfood isn't a staple around here." He wasn't used to early morning conversation with anyone, but Dakota was proving it wasn't all bad. He was rather enjoying it.

"I was going to ask you if we could go into town and pick something up for him."

"Absolutely."

As much as Colt hated to ruin the moment, he had a job to do that centered around her today, and none of the job included fun and games.

They had Mateo's office bugged, but Dakota apparently knew a little more of his habits and had managed to secure vital information as a result. Information he and Jack had missed.

"I need to talk to you about today. What would you need to set up here to listen in at Victor's?"

"My computer. It's in my car. Oh, and my purse is still in the car, too. I don't want it stolen."

"Here's the deal. You have taps in Mateo's home. We do, too, but I must admit you have them in better places, because we missed the change in plans last night."

"I didn't admit to that, but, in light of our arrangement, I will tell you I know where he goes for privacy in his own home. Unless you've been hanging out with him personally, they are places you wouldn't know. I did have a plan all along. Just one that didn't include the FBI showing up."

The thought of her in Mateo's house alone made him tense. "It was dangerous. You were as good as dead if you got caught." It was the other reason he'd agreed to the five minutes. He was just getting to know Dakota, but it hadn't taken him long to figure out she'd have gone right back to Mateo's house another night to get what she was after. It was better for them both if she had his protection. After she got what she wanted, it would put an end to her madness.

"I wasn't going to get caught." Her chin jutted up in defiance.

He cast her a disparaging look. "You did get caught."

"But not by Victor."

"Give it up. You won't win this one. Not with me."

"Fine. It was dangerous. Happy? But the next time, it won't be dangerous because you'll have him under lock and key, and he'll never know I was there. There will be no way for him to connect me to the missing jewelry."

"First, we need to find out when he's going to move the Wingate jewels."

"The Wingate jewels? You suspect Mateo stole them? They are amazing. I saw them once when they were on loan at the museum in San Francisco."

"We think he stole them from the duchess when she was visiting New York. It looked as though he was going to fence them the night we caught you."

"Ah, I see. And then lady love got in the way. Evelyn Madding can be very persuasive."

"Apparently," he said dryly. "It would be great if you could pull up your taps and listen, just in case you can get lucky twice."

"Lucky my butt. I knew exactly what I was doing. I'll agree, but only because you're going to cover for me. We need my computer out of the car, so the sooner we head over there, the sooner I can check my machine and hook it up so we can listen to it live."

"How exactly do you intend to get the jewelry?" Colt asked, almost afraid of the answer.

"I learned how to crack a safe." She looked like a cat who just finished a big bowl of cream. *Catwoman.*

"Oh, please. I didn't need to know that. Forget I asked." He shook his head, trying to dispel the image of her breaking into Victor's safe.

"Well, how did you think I would open the safe in Victor's study?" Dakota shrugged, as if it were no big deal.

Agreeing to give her five minutes was one thing, giving her five minutes to commit a crime was another. "I was hoping you had the combination by some stroke of good luck."

"Nope. Sorry to disappoint. I'll open it the good old-fashioned way. Click by click."

"And you think five minutes is enough?" This woman was incredibly brave or incredibly foolish. Time would tell which.

"Yup. After I saw Victor with the locket, I contacted a local, um, expert, and described the safe I saw. The guy helped me to understand the mechanics of the lock and I've been practicing. I'm going to get my mother's locket back and find out what else Victor still has of hers, and nothing will stop me until I do."

That's what he was afraid of. "About that..." Colt drawled out. He didn't know if Dakota knew much about her parents or if this would be like dropping a bomb, but either way, it had to be done. "Did you know your mother and Victor used to date in high school?"

Her eyes darkened. "How could you say such a vile thing. You're wrong. She would have *never* dated someone like him. Besides, my dad always said they got together in high school and that he never had eyes for anyone else. They had a beautiful love, and I don't appreciate you trying to tarnish it." Her back was ramrod straight, the tension between them palatable. Halo had gone back to her and began nudging her hand, trying to get her attention.

"That doesn't prove she didn't date Victor first." Dakota could deny it all she wanted. The facts were there and easily confirmed. "In fact, they were king and queen at their prom."

"My mom and dad, right?" Her eyes narrowed; disbelief written on her face.

"Victor and your mom." It was a truth that Dakota needed to know. He just hated being the one that had to tell her.

She shook her head, tears welling up in her eyes.

"I'm sorry, Dakota." And he was, but the truth had to come out if they were going to find out what happened the night her parents died.

"So, what's your point?" Her hostile gaze pinned him with their intensity.

"I'm looking for a motive."

Her eyes flew wide open. "What? Does that mean you believe me?" The hostility was instantly replaced by a look of hope.

"I'm trying to, but there are a few problems with your version of what happened." He'd already said more than he should have, but if they were going to work together, it would be easier to lay it on the line with her. "First, the burglary report made no mention of the tattoo. Why do you think that is? Are you sure there was a man with a tattoo, or has the tattoo become a new development with your recent memory reversal?"

"*Arghh.* You're the most infuriating man. Either you believe me, or you don't. I don't have a clue why they didn't list it. It's not like I ever got to see the report. I was twelve." Her eyes burned into him. "And just because I couldn't remember what the tattoo looked like doesn't mean I didn't see it. They didn't believe me, did they? Everyone thought I made it all up." She closed her eyes and rubbed her forehead as if the pain was too much too bear.

"That's one possibility." Colt answered truthfully.

"Thanks for looking into the case." Her shoulders slumped dejectedly. "Even if you won't admit it, I think deep down you believe me, otherwise you wouldn't have gone to the effort to find all this out. Would you?"

"I told you, I deal in facts. Don't confuse me looking into the two cases as anything more than it is. A review of the facts." He didn't want to get her hopes up for nothing.

"It's all I can ask." Dakota stood and crossed the room to his side.

"Thank you," she said, her voice soft and velvety. Her hand reached up to touch his cheek, the soft flesh of her palm cupping his face.

His heart hammered in his chest. It took every inch of will power he possessed not to kiss her, but if he did, where would it stop? And it would be crossing professional lines he'd never crossed before. His by-the-book methods had only recently come into question with the arrival of Dakota on the scene. But once was more than enough.

"This isn't a good idea." He stepped back, out of her reach.

"You're probably right. I'm just trying to show my appreciation for your efforts. Don't confuse it with anything else. Thanks for talking to me and trying to figure out what happened, but I understand. Business is business."

"Exactly. And I can't mix business and pleasure." With so much up in the air and yet to be solved, the one thing he knew for certain was that kissing Dakota would be all pleasure.

Chapter Seven

♥

THEY PULLED INTO THE parking lot of the RCPD, and Dakota spotted her Mustang. "There's Matilda." She pointed to the rear of the parking area.

"Do you have your keys?" Colt asked, pulling up behind the car and blocking her in.

"Of course." She dug them out of her backpack and opened the car door.

"Grab your things and let's get out of here," Colt ordered in his do-it-my-way voice. A voice she'd grown used to since meeting him.

"And leave the car? Are you crazy?"

"I can have one of the guys drive it over to the house in the morning if you give me your key. I'll leave it with the front desk."

She got out of the car, and Colt followed, not letting her get too far on her own. He had her blocked in for goodness sake, exactly where did he think she would go? Not to mention, Halo was back at the house waiting on her and breakfast. Dakota wasn't the one calling the shots.

Any warm feelings she had for the guy disappeared as she got her computer and purse out of the car, locked it back up, and handed him the key. "Nothing better happen to my car, or you'll pay. There's not a scratch on her, so I'll know."

"It's just a car."

"You're wrong. My father bought this car for my mother not long after I was born. They'd given up hope of ever having a baby and always called me their little miracle. We used to go for family rides in it down to Cliff Walk to watch the whales and ride along the coast. Some of my best memories are tied to that car. My aunt and uncle saved it for me until I was old enough to drive." It had been the best gift a sixteen-year-old could get. Some her friends got new cars, but she wouldn't trade Matilda for any of them.

"I'm sorry. I didn't know." Colt's hand touched her shoulder lightly, his eyes echoing the sentiment. "It still has to be done my way. You know I want to believe you, but there is still a part of me that doesn't have the answers I need to make the pieces fit. Part of it being you're conveniently a gemologist and Victor's a jewel thief. An unlikely combo in any book unless something else is going on. Coincidence or convenient?"

She winced. Colt was using her words against her. "I explained the something else." Dakota groaned in frustration.

"I know, but until I have proof, I have to do my job. And that means keeping a close eye on you until this case is closed."

"I see." Or at least she was trying to. At times, she thought he liked having her around. But it really was just his job, and she'd be a fool to start imaging anything else existed between them.

"No, you probably don't, judging by your tone." Colt pulled open the passenger door for her to get in his car. "Wait here. I'll be back in two minutes. If you're not here, our deal is off, and I'll issue an arrest warrant to make sure you don't get far. Understood?"

"Yes, sir, sergeant, sir." It's not like she could go anywhere with no car. "Do you mind if I call my aunt and uncle? They'll be worried because I didn't come home last night." Dakota pulled her cell phone from her purse.

It was her day off today, and technically, she didn't have to call in her whereabouts, but since she was still living with them, she did it out of respect. They were the only family she had, and she loved them unconditionally. She was grateful they'd taken her in and treated her like a daughter after the tragedy. She looked up at Colt for approval when he didn't answer right away.

"Okay. But remember, not a word about Victor, or the FBI, and that includes me." Colt thought of everything, or at least he tried to.

She hoped he applied the same principles when it came to search out the truth about her parents.

"Not a word. I promise. Anything else?" Colt might not trust her completely, but she wasn't stupid. Telling her aunt and uncle would start a maelstrom of events, none of which would bring her the satisfaction she craved of getting her mother's jewelry back and bringing Victor to justice. They led a quiet life, one that focused on running the business, and not chasing down criminals or breaking and entering someone's house to steal what rightfully belonged to her. It was something she'd decided to do on her own, and that hadn't changed.

"Nope. That'll do." He turned and headed up the steps of the station.

Dakota pressed the speed dial for her aunt. She didn't have to wait long. "Hey, Aunt Mary. Just thought I should check in."

"Good heavens, girl. Where are you? I've been worried since you didn't come home last night."

"I'm fine. It got late, and I decided to stay with a friend. I knew you'd be in bed, and it was too late to call. Sorry."

"Your Uncle Fred said as much, but men don't worry enough. I couldn't put much stock in his words."

Dakota knew a guy just the opposite. Colt was a worrier. "Well, he was right this time. Halo's with me, and I'm thinking of staying with my friend another day or two. I was hoping Uncle Frank would cover my shift at the store tomorrow."

"*Hmmm*. This isn't like you. Who's the friend? Not some boy you just met, is it?" Her aunt's brisk disapproval was loud and clear.

Dakota swallowed hard. "No, Aunt Mary. It's a friend I met in San Francisco at the conference. It'll be fine. I'm going to stop and pick up some food for Halo. He's having fun." She hated lying to her aunt, but there was no other choice. For her own sake, and because she'd promised Colt. Besides, it wasn't like she way shacking up with a boy she liked. This was all business. And Colt was all man, not a boy—not that her aunt needed to know that information.

"Okay, if you say so. I'm sure Frank won't mind. He's always at the store anyway. He's so afraid he's going to miss a sale, or worse, an important client. He loves to talk, that man does." Aunt Mary laughed.

Aunt Mary was a talker as well, which made the two of them a great couple. Like her parents had been. "Thanks. I'll keep you posted when I'm coming home. Talk to you later." She disconnected without waiting for answer, not wanting to prolong the conversation and take a chance of tripping up.

Colt slid in the car seconds after she hung up. "Everything okay?"

"Peachy. I told my aunt I'm shacking up with a hot hunk and not to expect me home for a few days. She said have fun." Dakota shook her head and laughed.

"Very funny. But I'm glad you cleared the air for a few days. There's no telling how long this will take."

"Don't sound so put out by it. It was your decision to keep me a prisoner. Don't forget to stop for dog food. If you stick to the outskirts of town, we stand a better chance of no one recognizing me. I told Aunt Mary I was down in the San Francisco area."

"Wow. You are good at the lying thing. Should I worry?" Colt was the one grinning now.

"Touché. Nice touch. Now drive. My dog is hungry and waiting for me." Or more likely sleeping. It was Dakota who needed Halo to give her the courage to continue this plan. Her canine companion knew just how to calm her, and right now, she needed lots of calming. Mostly because of her torn feelings for the man sitting next to her. She'd be a fool to let herself care, but every hour they spent together drew him closer into a circle she'd never let anyone break into previously.

Colt drove to the store. As if by some unspoken agreement, they managed to only make small talk, steering clear of Victor, the jewels, and the crash. Which was fine with her. Colt went inside the store and bought what she told him to get. By the time they arrived at his house, Halo was dancing by the front door, needing a potty break and food, in that order.

The rest of the day followed much the same pattern of conversation. Small talk. Get-to-know-you conversation, only it seemed she was the one doing most of the talking. Colt Jackson, it turned out, wasn't much of talker. Unless it pertained to FBI business. Then he had lots to say.

Dakota stayed in the kitchen, listening to the bugs she had in place at Victor's. He had yet to make an appearance, keeping things on the boring side of life.

Colt hovered close by, only leaving the room a few times. How could he not trust her yet? And what did she need to do to earn it? She trusted him. Or at the very least, his badge. Colt was a sexy, tough guy with a twist. The man who fearlessly went after criminals for a living was afraid of dogs. Halo, on the other hand, had no problem with Colt whatsoever, going out of his way to sidle up next to him, looking to make a friend.

Between exaggerated sighs, long, hard looks, frequent pacing, and hard tapping on the keyboard of his computer, the man was otherwise an enigma. She would have loved to get inside his head and find out what he was thinking. Each time he stopped pacing or to look up from his computer, she felt he was on the verge of saying something, but then nothing. Silence.

A couple of hours passed, and soon, Dakota had enough. "Any idea what to do for lunch, since I'm guessing you're not overly stocked?" she asked, forcing him to answer.

He stopped typing long enough to look up from the computer and consider her question. "I can have a pizza delivered, if that's okay. I don't cook."

"We should have gone in together at the convenience store and picked something up. Maybe we could go now and get some things and then I could cook for you." The idea of him sitting alone night after night eating take-out food or frozen dinners tugged at her heart.

"Or not. We need to stay here and listen in case Victor contacts anyone important." Always the voice of reason. His job must have some exciting parts to make up for putting up with something so mundane and boring as sitting around and doing nothing.

"You're no fun, and I was just trying to be nice," she teased, trying to get him to talk.

"This is a job. It's not supposed to be fun, but thanks for the offer. Maybe some other time when this is over, and if you're not seeing any-one." Colt's steadfast gaze held hers. Her breath caught. Did he mean it?

Dakota frowned. *If you're not seeing any-one.* He couldn't possibly still think of her and Victor as being a couple. His double-edged comment was both shocking and irritating. She thought they were passed this.

"Seriously? I'm going to tell you this for the last time, mister, so listen up. After I saw the picture of Victor and Evelyn in the paper, I purposely set out to arrange to be in a place where he might notice me. I look a lot alike my mother and hoped he would remember me and strike up a conversation. It worked. For the past couple of months, I've gone to his house with the purpose of getting information and trying to find out if any of my mother's jewelry is still in his possession. Victor has treated me more like a daughter than a woman he wants to hook up with. And don't forget...he's a criminal. Do I look desperate to you?"

"No. You're gorgeous. But I can't imagine any man being around you and not wanting to sleep with you. So forgive me if I tend to think Victor's interest in you has been more than platonic. And for the record, it isn't only Victor I'm concerned about." Colt closed the distance between them with each word he uttered until he came to a stop inches away from her. "Are you? Dating someone, that is?" His voice ground out, low and possessive.

Dakota was speechless. Nothing out of the man all morning and then, bam!

A warm, fuzzy feeling washed over every inch of her body. She didn't care about other men, but she did care about Colt. He was an interesting mix of commanding, funny, determined, sexy, and caring. And she wanted to know more. But could she believe him? Her track record with men wasn't that great.

Whether he believed it or not, she had morals. Very high morals, truth be told. Of course, living with her aunt and uncle didn't make it easy to have guys over for a hot date, so it wasn't like the opportunities were endless, the way Colt seemed to think.

Dakota struggled for an answer, but nothing came to her. A crackling noise sounded from her computer, the microphones picking up sound. Saved by a bug.

A door slammed.

Colt didn't say a word but followed her over to the computer, where they sat side-by-side to listen.

The scuff of a chair.

She had two bugs in the room. It didn't matter where Victor stood, she should be able to hear anything said in the room. But it was the one in the alcove she wanted to come to life. A strategically placed fish tank and the sound of the pump afforded him privacy if anyone happened to be in the room when he was on the phone, and it was exactly the reason she'd put a bug there.

Colt's woodsy scent made it hard to concentrate. Sooner or later, he'd ask her the question again, and she'd better have a ready answer the second time.

Other than the rustling of papers and an occasional cough, the next hour netted them nothing. She was tired and stood to stretch.

"I'll call in for in pizza. You keep listening," Colt ordered.

"Yes, sir, sergeant, sir." Dakota knew he'd hated it when she'd said it once before, and she couldn't resist teasing him now. Anything for fun to break up the monotony.

"Very funny. But I'm on to you now, and it won't work. Your teasing, that is."

"Go order the pizza and leave me alone." She turned away to smile, not wanting to lay all her cards out for him to inspect and decipher. He knew too much about her as it was.

Twenty minutes later, the doorbell rang, and Colt left to pay for the pizza. He returned with the pizza and a bottle of wine tucked under his arm. He set their dinner on the table and grabbed two wineglasses.

"*Mmmm.* Smells good." Dakota was starved. Halo looked up and sniffed the air. "Sorry, boy. You need to wait 'til dinner for more food. Can't have you packing on the pounds."

"I'm guessing he doesn't get people food?"

"Nope. Carol, the woman I got him from, is very selective about who gets her puppies and is adamant they are trained and fed correctly. It comes in handy, trust me."

"What do you mean?" Colt grabbed two plates and some napkins before sitting down next to her.

"I volunteer over at the Redwood Cove Nursing and Rehab Center. Halo's allowed inside because he's a therapy dog, so I take him over to meet with the patients on Thursdays."

"But what's that got to do with people food? Even as a treat."

"Because people eat people food, and if Halo ate people food, he'd be taking it right off their plates. That would get him kicked out in a hurry." Dakota enjoyed helping the others and was grateful Halo's gift was useful to so many others who needed comfort.

Colt laughed, the sound not one she heard often enough. "Are you going to answer my question or avoid it all night long?" He turned serious on her in a split second.

"I'd forgotten you asked." *Liar.* "I'm not seeing anyone. And I'd like to cook you a nice meal when all this is finished." There, she'd said it. It had come out easier than she'd thought it would. Probably because of Halo. Or maybe because of Colt. It was an interesting thought. The whole meaning of surveillance changed with Colt sitting in knee-touching distance. Even if it was unintentional.

"Good. It's a date." Colt sat back in his chair, a satisfied grin on his face. "Any updates?"

"You were gone five minutes." She shook her head in frustration. How could they go from a discussion about dating to one that emphasized his lack of trust in her?

"It's business, Dakota. Many a man who let their guard down ends up dead in my line of work. It's not that I *don't* trust you." His emphasis on the word *don't* was clear.

"But it's not that you trust me, either."

"A distinction with a difference. And an important one as far as we are concerned."

"We?"

"You and me."

"There isn't a you and me as far as I know." She had just agreed to a date, but one date didn't make a relationship.

"Not at the moment anyway," he said, before stuffing another big bite of pizza in his mouth.

"If we're going to have this one date, maybe I should know more about you than I do now. I know you're an FBI agent, single, you don't trust me, and you don't like dogs. Which by the way, is a deal breaker for anything beyond a friendly thank-you date. I'm hoping I'm wrong about that part." It was better to ask up front, because Halo wasn't going anywhere.

"There's not much to tell. I've been an agent for eight years, and I move around a lot. This isn't my house. It's a rental courtesy of the government for as long as this assignment lasts." Colt shrugged and sat back in his chair.

"Well, that explains the non-personal aspect of the place a lot better than your original version. Does it get old? The moving around part, that is. Why'd you become an agent?" They were finally talking, and she was determined to learn everything she could about him.

"Of course, it gets old. But it's my job. I grew up in a rough area outside Los Angeles and wanted to make a difference. I saw a lot as a young kid that wasn't pretty." Colt brushed a crumb off his jeans. "And for the record, I do trust you. I'm following protocol, to make sure there's backup if my trust is misplaced."

"Okay, okay. I get it. What about the dog part? Do you, or don't you?" She held her breath, waiting to hear it directly from Colt.

"Like dogs? I'm okay with them. Not a big fan, but I deal. Most of the time." His non-committal answer spoke volumes.

"What happened?" She knew there must be a story. Most people who didn't like dogs had had a bad experience, and she wanted to know his.

"Who says anything happened?" Colt stopped eating, tossing his pizza onto the plate. He reached for his wine and took a sip.

"You. Your actions. Little things I've noticed here and there."

A look of resignation crossed his face. "Let's just say a big, mean dog tried to change my life. As in, end it." Colt rubbed his neck as if talking about the incident made him uncomfortable.

"Oh my. I'm so sorry. Was it in the line of duty?" She reached out to touch his arm, offering comfort much the same way Halo did for her. Touch was a powerful medicine.

"Yes. Jack saved my life."

"No wonder Halo keeps trying to reach out to you. He's trying to connect. I started to wonder when he was doing the head nudges to you. He won't hurt you; I promise."

"Yeah, well, I'm good. It's easier just to keep my distance."

"Halo, here boy." Dakota snapped her fingers, and Halo was by her side.

"You don't listen well, do you?" Colt asked, a frown on his face.

"Just pet him. Let him lick your hand. Smell you. You'll see what I mean."

After several seconds, Colt reached out, tentative at first. Halo nudged his hand. Colt never took his eyes off the dog, stroking him behind the ears but keeping his hand well away from the dog's mouth.

Dakota wouldn't push him to do more. Halo was in full control and in therapy mode, bumping Colt's hand to get the best contact for a neck rub. Her therapy dog was just as much in this for himself as he was for her. Dakota laughed.

There was hope for Colt and Halo. Dakota wasn't about to write the man out of the picture quite yet. After a few long, quiet minutes, she broke the silence. "What about women?"

"What about women?" He looked up at her in confusion.

"It must be hard for you to date if you're always moving around?" His file was full of information on her, and it was only fair she got more details.

Colt looked at her sharply, pulling his hand away from Halo. And just like before, Dakota sensed there had to be a story.

"You ask a lot of questions. Eat your pizza." Secret code for she wasn't going to find out. "And try to get some of it in your mouth." He smiled, softening his abrupt response and reaching over to wipe whatever was clinging to her cheek.

The touch of his fingers distracted her.

Almost. The man was a master at evasion, but not this time. "Nice try. You asked me about

men in my life, what about women in yours?"
she persisted.

"There are none. By choice. If I want anything, it's not hard to find a no-strings-attached
woman. Is that what you wanted to hear?" His
voice had turned sarcastic and completely out of
character.

This wasn't the Colt she'd come to know, and
she wasn't letting him off the hook that easily.
"Well, no. Not really. Do you avoid relationships
because of your job, or do you avoid them because there's a history?"

He shot her a hard look. "Both. Let it go,
Dakota."

Whatever it was, he didn't want to talk about
it, and Halo's response to him was a good in-
dicator whatever ailed him went deep. Dakota
also noticed him absently stroking Halo's head.
"Fine, for now."

"What about you? You said you're not dating
anyone right now, and you insist you're not Victor's play toy of the month, so is there a history

you want to talk about?" He was being mean on purpose.

She ignored the barbed comment. "Like you mentioned earlier, it's a little hard living at home. But maybe it's time to rectify the situation. On both accounts." She shoved back her chair and stood. "I'm sure someone would be all too happy to oblige. I'm taking the dog outside to pee, unless that's not in your handbook of rules."

Colt frowned. "I hardly—" The sound of a chair scraping across the floor again drew their attention back to the computer. Victor's phone rang.

It reminded her of exactly why she was here with Colt Jackson. She'd put everything on the line to get her mother's jewelry back and to put Victor behind bars. And the man next to her could make it all happen. She'd be a fool to get involved before or after Victor was behind bars. It was one thing to have a relationship fall apart after a short time, quite another to go into one *knowing* it would end. And Colt was making that part clear. He was a loner by choice.

"Victor." Victor's voice came through the speaker with crystal clarity. "My terms are five million. All hundreds. Blue canvas duffle bag. My place. Alone. And Antonio...you'll have to go through the metal detector at the front door, so no monkey business. Come unarmed."

Dakota would give anything to know what was being said on the other end of the line.

"Yes. Eight-fifteen tomorrow night. I expect you to be punctual." Another pause.

"The jewels are safe with me until then, no worries. Later." Victor hung up the phone.

They both let out the breath they'd been holding. Overjoyed, Dakota launched herself into Colt's arms, wrapping her arms around his neck. So much for trying to keep everything all business. "We got him!"

"And hopefully, no change of plans this time." Colt grinned, his arms coming around her waist.

"Should have taken me on as a partner," she teased, their heads only inches apart.

"Obviously." Dakota watched with anticipation as Colt lowered his mouth toward her waiting lips. She'd think about her *no-Colt* decision later.

Except the kiss never came.

Colt pulled back at the last second, leaving her bereft of the warmth of his lips and the expectation of something wonderful. "Business," he grumbled before turning away and headed for the door.

"Colt?" She couldn't keep the hurt of his rejection from her voice.

He turned back. "We can't. You're under government protection. It goes against everything I stand for. I'm sorry. Tomorrow, I'll get you a bracelet, and we'll make plans. I've got to call Jack and get the ball rolling."

"Bracelet?" *Why would he get her a bracelet? Maybe he did care more than he let on.*

"A tracking bracelet. In case you get any ideas." She'd forgotten that part of their deal.

"Overbearing jerk," she grumbled.

Chapter Eight

♥

COLT SHOULD HAVE NEVER agreed to Dakota's crazy proposal in the first place, but somewhere along the way, he'd decided he wasn't going to change mind. And if she could produce her mother's jewelry, it would give him the probable cause he needed to reopen the accident case.

Unfortunately, her possession of them would keep him from pressing charges against Mateo for the burglary without further proof. Murder was a far more serious charge anyway. Colt's butt was on the line if anything went wrong, so he intended to make sure everything went right. It wasn't like he had any other good options.

Dakota was as determined as she was feisty. He leveled her with a hard look, hoping to make her understand the danger. "Remember everything we've gone over. I haven't said a word to Jack about what you're going to be doing after we grab Mateo, and I'd like to keep it that way. He thinks the sole reason I'm dragging you along is to keep you from ratting us out to him. The less everyone knows about your connection to Mateo and your special safecracking skill, the better for both of us."

"I'm grateful you agreed to let me do this, Colt, and I know it can get you in trouble. I promise to do everything just as we planned." Halo came up to sit by her feet and dropped his leash. She reached down to pet him.

"Then make sure you stay completely hidden until the coast is clear. The last thing I need is for you to get hurt and me to have to explain to everyone why I didn't just put you in protective custody under the guard of another agent." There was still time to change his mind, but he wouldn't do that to her. She deserved this chance to right some wrongs.

"Yes, sir, sergeant, sir," she retorted, the twinkle in her eye taking out the sting. Halo nudged her hand.

"Sorry, boy. I'm not sure you can go with me this time." She glanced up at him, looking for confirmation.

"No can do. I have enough to worry about as it is. If you feel yourself on edge, just let me know, and I'll be there to help you if I can."

"Okay. I trust you." Dakota knelt beside the dog and rubbed his head, reassuring him as well as herself. The calming effect on them both was remarkable. Colt had never seen this type of bond between a dog and its owner. It was like some sort of silent communication existed between them. She picked up his leash and hooked it on his collar.

"One other thing," he said, reaching into his pocket and pulling out the silver bracelet he'd put there earlier. He'd put off strapping it on Dakota for as long as he could, enjoying the camaraderie they'd been sharing. He was loath to end it, but he held the bracelet out for her inspection. "The guys from headquarters delivered it this morning per my request. Looks just like a regular bracelet, so you won't feel like a criminal." He smiled, hoping to soften the impact.

"It's very pretty but doesn't say much for the trust you claim to have. I still prefer not to wear it." Her face was scrunched up in distaste, but he drew the line on this point.

"No bracelet, no trip to Mateo's." He shrugged. "I can have one of our guys here in ten minutes to collect you. The choice is yours."

"I'm not a piece of baggage, and I'm not a criminal," she huffed, her hands firmly planted on her hips.

Colt chuckled, liking her feisty attitude. "Do I need to call the guys? We need to get a move on. Jack will be here any minute to pick us up, and you still need to take Halo out back for a minute."

"Fine." Dakota held out her arm.

Colt clasped the bracelet around her wrist, tightened it, and pocketed the key.

"Custom fit." He grinned. "I'll know every move you make right down to how fast you're walking or running, where you stop, and everything else in between. Make sure no one sees or hears you other than me or Jack." It was better to cover all the bases with Dakota before she got any ideas. His career, or at least his reputation, was hanging in the balance based on the way things went down tonight. He hoped he was putting his faith and trust in the right place.

"I keep telling you—"

"You're not working with Mateo. I know. But who's to say you're not working solo. You'd be the prettiest thief I've ever met, but in the end, the jewels would still end up missing. There's an awful lot of temptation floating around the Mateo residence." He watched her closely for any sign of striking a nerve, but there wasn't so much as a twitch or a flick of an eye.

Dakota opened the back door and led Halo into the back yard, Colt right behind her.

"You've been wrong before. How do you know he has the Wingate jewels?"

Leave it to Dakota to remind him about the bug deficiency in Victor's study. "Because we have people in places who hear things. Credible witnesses. Victor's fencing the jewels for half of what they're worth. We already placed him in the vicinity of the crime scene, and now he's trying to make a quick buck dumping the stolen property. Antonio is just a middleman. What we don't know is who the final buyer is, and if the Wingate collection slips through the cracks, they may disappear forever." The feds don't need any more heat for things going wrong on their watch."

"Okay, then let's do this." She finished letting Halo sniff around and do his business and then led him back inside. "Let me get him some water and then I'll be ready to go."

She picked up the dog bowl and crossed to the sink to fill it.

"We can't go until you change. I need you invisible, Catwoman." Nothing would make her invisible to him in the black outfit, but it was the surest way to make her blend in with the dark drapes in Mateo's study.

Setting the bowl back on the floor, she turned to him. "Fine. I told you I knew what I was doing the other night. Now that you've let the cat out of the bag—pun intended—you can just admit I'm good." The grin she shot him required no validation, her confidence at an all-time high.

Colt put a call through to Jack. "Hey there. Give us five minutes and pick us up out front."

"You sure about this, Colt? Taking her along is dangerous, and definitely not in the procedure manual."

"I know, but believe me, it's for the best."

"Okay, you're the boss on this one. Just don't say I didn't warn you."

"Duly warned. Now get over here and let's get this done." Colt hung up and paced the room, Halo pacing with him. Strange dog.

Dakota pulled at the nylon material, trying to stretch it the best she could. It was one thing putting on the skin-tight outfit knowing no one would see her, entirely another to realize Colt was in the living room waiting to inspect her appearance. He'd ripped the threads that secured the masked to the outfit, but she pulled it on just the same, not wanting anyone to recognize her.

Taking a deep breath, she headed down the hall.

Colt stopped and turned as she entered the room, his gaze locking on her as if transfixed.

He'd also changed clothes. His black jeans molded his lower body, while the black T-shirt stretched tightly across his chest, revealing the contours of his abs and biceps. She couldn't help the rush of interest that filled her.

"Nice outfit." Colt grinned.

"Thanks. I put it on just for you." His eyes flared, causing Dakota to chuckle. "Not," she teased.

A horn honked. "That's Jack. Let's go." He pointed toward the side door in the kitchen.

"I asked him to pull up close to the garage so no one would see you in your outfit and get suspicious. The last thing we need is some nosy neighbor calling the cops."

She followed him to the garage, Halo right behind her. "Sorry, boy. You need to stay. I have my orders, but we'll be back soon. I promise." She rubbed his back and dropped a kiss on his head.

The first thing Dakota noticed was her car. "You didn't tell me they delivered my Mustang."

"Didn't want you to get any ideas." Lord, but the man could be the most irritating pain in the behind she'd ever met. "Not a scratch on it. I checked."

"Thanks, but I think I'll take a look for myself." Dakota walked around the car, letting her hand trail lovingly across the metal.

"Suit yourself but hurry it up. We need to leave." Colt shot her a hard look and pressed the button to open the automatic door.

Jack jumped out of the driver's seat and gave a low whistle. "Catwoman in action. So, which one of us is Batman, and which one is the Joker?" Jack chuckled.

"Well, since you're both supposed to be the good guys, and there's only one Batman, I guess that role should be yours, Jack." Dakota grinned, loving the stunned look on Colt's face. "You," she said, pressing her finger against Colt's chest to make her point, "are definitely a joker."

"Feisty and beautiful. Boy, did you luck out." Jack slapped Colt on the shoulder before moving to the van to slide open the side door.

"Nothing lucky about it." Coming from Colt, it didn't sound like a compliment. He was the one adamant about the professional status of their relationship, not her.

Dakota climbed into the van and buckled up, the guys sitting up front. It gave her time to think, because whether Colt knew it or not, entering Victor's house wasn't high on her priority list. Truth was, she was terrified. Although she hadn't said a thing to her temporary partner in crime, she was relieved to have two such hulking males by her side for protection. The last time, she'd been a bag of quivering nerves, terrified of Victor coming home unexpectedly, or any other disaster that could have occurred.

Colt thought she was brave or crazy, but the truth was, she was neither. She wanted her mother's jewelry back, and she wanted the man she was certain was responsible for their deaths, behind bars. She owed it to her parents. Revenge and justice drove her to do what she did, not bravery.

"Park in the same place as last time. We'll proceed just like before, except Catwoman here stays with me to keep her out of trouble," Colt ordered. It was more than clear he was in charge and expected his orders to be followed without question.

"More likely she's convinced you to let her back in to get what she was after the first time. Who do you think you're kidding? She got to you, bro." Jack laughed.

"That would be against protocol." Colt had turned defensive.

"Sure thing. Protocol, huh? That's how you want to play this?" Jack countered. He was clearly a non-believer, and rightly so. Jack knew his part all too well, but she was staying out of the fray. It was up to Colt to decide what he told his partner, but she'd give anything to see Colt's face. She had a feeling the man didn't let much rattle him.

"We're here," Colt said, ending the discussion. "The surveillance team reported Mateo left the house about twenty minutes ago. They tailed him to the Madding residence and will alert us when he's on the move again. He's got to be back here by eight-fifteen. We'll go through the same bedroom window Dakota used before. The trellis is the easiest way to get in. Let's just hope the window is still unlocked."

Dakota stayed close by his side. Colt reached out tentatively and then dropped his hand. "You going to be okay?"

"Yes, but thanks for checking."

"Jack, you're on the inside with us tonight. I've got another guy watching the front of the house in case anything goes wrong and Mateo shows up before we expect him or if we have any other unexpected visitors." He shot her a pointed look, remembering all too clearly the last time they were here.

Colt headed up the trellis first, Dakota close on his heels. She climbed using her hands and feet to coordinate the moves. At the top, Colt helped pull her inside. The moonlight cast a warm light in the room, making it easy to move around without bumping into furniture. At the door, Colt drew his gun and waved them down the hall.

Dakota froze. Her legs wouldn't move. The moonlight grazed the steel shaft and a vision of the past swamped her. She closed her eyes to block out the vision. Sucking in a deep breath, she tried to drive away the images.

Colt must have sensed her panic, because suddenly she was in his arms. "It's okay. I'm sorry," he whispered. "It's the gun, isn't it?"

Dakota nodded, feeling him move his arm behind his back. Seconds later, with one arm holding her tightly and the other running down the back of her hair, he tried to comfort her. "It's okay. You can open your eyes, I put it away."

"If you two are quite through, you do realize where we are and what's at stake, right?" Jack crawled through the window. "Save the lovey-dovey stuff for when this is over."

"It's not what you think, so can it. I'll explain later," Colt snapped.

He leaned his head down lower to hers. "Are you going to be okay? We need to get a move on, or get you the heck out of here."

"No. Let's do this," she said, her voice trembling.

"It won't be dark in the room when Victor arrives, and I'll be right there. I won't let anything happen to you."

She smiled up at him. "I believe you. I believe in you," she reiterated.

"Good girl. Let's go."

"It's about time," Jack mumbled.

They eased down the hallway toward Victor's office. Colt nudged her arm and pointed to the drapes—her cue to make herself scarce. He spoke into his headset, his voice low and almost indiscernible.

"Mateo's out front." Colt ground out in a low voice.

"Roger that," Jack answered before stepping off to the side to get into position behind the door.

Hidden behind the drapes was all too much like a repeat of history—like she was twelve again. The only different was these were dark and sinister, the black brocade thick like a cloak. She tried to focus on the spot where she knew Colt was hidden, instead of letting her memories drag her down the forbidden path. It was one thing to sneak in and steal back her mother's jewelry when she knew Victor was out for the evening, quite another to do it when he was home.

It was a long fifteen minutes before Victor entered his office. Dakota didn't dare look or move for fear of discovery. A chair scraped against the floor, followed by the leather seat creaking as someone sat down. A drawer was opened and closed.

Within minutes, the doorbell rang. Victor's chair scraped back, his footsteps crossed the room and then the door closed. She didn't hear a sound for at least a minute, and she finally dared to sneak a look into the well-lit room. The light helped settle her nerves and warded off the panic attack she'd been desperately fighting against. She took several deep breaths, trying to relax.

Voices sounded from below, and then heavy footsteps sounded on the stairs, matching the sound of her heart thumping in her chest. This was it. She swallowed hard. She wondered how Colt and Jack could do this time and time again, putting their life on the line. They were brave men to be sure, but it must be a hard life.

The door opened and people entered. She assumed Victor and the man he'd referred to as Antonio.

"Five mil entitles me to a full preview before I hand over the cash," Antonio said.

"Sure. I have them ready for your inspection. I knew you would expect no less." Victor's voice crawled across her skin.

A drawer was pulled open and then something scraped against the surface of the desk. "Feel free to inspect them." The man was a snake, and Dakota was relieved to know that after tonight, Victor would be in jail where he belonged.

"The lighting in this room isn't ideal, but it will do. *Hmmm.* They are exactly as the pictures describe them, only more beautiful. Such deep, blood-red perfection." Antonio was all but drooling over what must be the Wingate collection.

"Let's make this quick, shall we?" *Yes, Victor. Make it quick.* It had only been minutes, but it felt like forever stuck behind the heavy brocade curtains.

"Yes. Yes. Of course. Very good. The cash is all there. Count it if you want."

Two long zippers were pulled back. "Looks good to me. I trust it's all there, and of course, I know where to find you if it isn't," Victor said, not a trace of humor in his voice. She shuddered to think of what he would do to someone if they double-crossed him.

"You know me better than that. Trust is a serious matter between men like us. I trust you, you trust me, and we're both happy." Antonio's warning was just as clear as Victor's. These men were in the big leagues and didn't play around.

"Freeze. FBI. Hands in the air," Colt and Jack shouted simultaneously.

Dakota couldn't help but steal a look from behind the edge of the curtain.

"What's the meaning of this?" Antonio hollered, his hands in the air.

Victor, on the other hand, grinned, but he failed to move otherwise.

Grinned. Odd reaction, to be sure.

"You're both being charged with the possession of stolen property and intent to sell and buy stolen property. Hands up, Mateo," Colt ordered again.

"There's no stolen property here. It's all legit. Bought and paid for," Victor countered defensively.

"The Wingate jewels were reported stolen, not sold. And since you're in possession of the jewels, that connects you to the crime." Colt addressed the men with a calm she wasn't feeling.

"Fine. Have it your way, but I want to make a call to my attorney."

"When you get to the station, you can make a call," Colt snapped.

Watching the FBI agents in action from her secret spot gave her a thrill she hadn't expected. It was almost empowering in an odd sort of way. Maybe she should have gone into law enforcement instead of gemology.

Jack and Colt slapped handcuffs on the men and radioed for backup. The two men never shut up, demanding their rights. Within minutes, the place was crawling with agents, the two men were read their rights and were led out of the room. Antonio left with a few choice curse words and hollered all the way down the stairs.

Victor was still smiling. Odd reaction for a man who just got arrested.

Colt rolled up the velvet cloth to secure the jewels and placed them in the black box on the desk. Jack grabbed up the canvas bag filled with the money and hoisted it over his shoulder. They weren't going anywhere without the valuables safely in their possession.

The cash and jewels were there for the taking if the agents wanted a piece of the action. *Or her.* She finally understood Colt's position in making her wear the tracker bracelet. Five million in cash and ten million dollars' worth of jewels would be an overwhelming temptation, and he didn't know her or her motives enough to withstand a fifteen-million-dollar carrot.

Jack and Colt headed for the door. Colt paused and looked back at her, holding up his fingers, giving her a five-minute reminder, and then they were gone.

Chapter Nine

❤

DAKOTA STEPPED OUT FROM behind the drapes and into the light. It seemed strange to be in Victor's office, out in the open, and in a well-lit room—but it would certainly make it easier. She didn't have time to waste, five minutes was all Colt promised.

She crossed the room to the grouping of five black-framed photos on the wall and removed the one on the upper left, revealing a small safe. It was a clever move, putting two safes in his office. The second one was small enough that no one would suspect or think to look for it after the other obvious choice. Jewels didn't take up much room, and it was all he needed to conceal them. Anyone else would break into the larger safe behind his desk—even Colt, for that matter, hadn't known the second one existed.

Dakota pulled the mask from her head, knowing it would be easier to listen to the lock tumblers falling into place. She grabbed the stethoscope from her bag and placed it next to the dial, slowly turning the knob to hear the resounding tell-tale double click of the wheel tab catching against the drive pin and dropping the fence into the wheel tumbler. She'd practiced this hundreds of times, but the pressure of knowing her watch was ticking off valuable seconds made it harder to concentrate.

Click. Click. Yes! Twenty-two. She mentally registered the number. Slowly, she turned the dial back in the opposite direction. Listening intently for any sound echoing from the internal chamber. *Click. Click.* Ninety. One number to go, and the hardest of all. Her hands shook as she turned the dial one notch at a time. She glanced at her watch. Two minutes to go.

Dakota swiped the back of her hand across her forehead and rubbed her eyes. She needed to concentrate. One full turn and nothing. She'd missed it.

Swirling the dial several times to clear the memory, she redialed, left to twenty-two, right to ninety. Turning the dial left again, she closed her eyes and tried to visualize the fence falling into place, waiting for the sound. She had to get it right. It would be her last chance.

Dakota opened her eyes to check her progress. Forty-two. She was running out of room. Sixty-seconds to go.

She couldn't fail her parents, not after all these years. Closing her eyes again, she took a deep breath and continued to turn the dial. Another inch and nothing. She was too close to passing the previous mark that would mean failure.

Click. Click. Her eyes shot open. Eighty-nine. No wonder she'd missed it the first time around. One number away made it almost impossible to decipher, but she'd done it. Twenty-seconds to spare. She turned the tiny lever and pulled open the safe. The inside was only big enough for the size of a man's hand to fit in, but it went deep. Deeper than she'd expected.

She instantly recognized the blue and gold intertwined scrolling across the top of the box at the front of the safe—her mother's. She remembered as a young girl thinking the jewels had to be worth millions and millions of dollars. They were more beautiful than anything she had ever seen. She'd asked her mother and had never forgotten the answer to her question.

"More valuable than that because your father gave them to me with his love. Love always conquers money. Never forget that sweetheart."

Dakota removed the top of the box and scanned the contents. A quick glance was all she could afford, but it brought relief. Incredibly, it appeared everything was here. She'd been worried he would have sold off the pieces one by one. Even her mother's locket had been put back in the box after she'd caught Victor looking at it.

Glancing at her watch, she realized she was out of time. There was another box at the back of the safe, but she had everything she'd come for. Stealing her own jewels didn't make her a thief. Stealing someone else's would. She quickly closed the safe and spun the dial. She picked up the photo from the floor and hurriedly replaced it.

Men's voices could be heard below in the foyer. Dakota pulled open the office door, peeked out, and then skirted down the hallway to the spare bedroom where they'd arrange to meet. She eased the door closed behind her and then hid in the darkened corner to wait.

She'd done it.

Her mother's most treasured possessions were back where they belonged—with Dakota. She kissed the box, a few tears trickling down her face.

The voices grew closer, disappearing into the office. A little too close for her liking. Colt had been adamant about her not being discovered. She hoped she'd remembered to put everything back exactly as she found it in her haste. The minutes dragged on like hours. It was all too much like a replay of the night she'd been trapped with Victor as a child.

She needed to move from the shadows into the light before the overwhelming sense of anxiety took over and she crumbled. The moonlight coming from the window drew her forward, allowing her to move without a sound or fear of bumping into anything.

Down below, a lone figure stood at the base of the trellis. Jack. Seeing him standing there gave her comfort. If he was out there waiting, Colt wouldn't be long now. Even as she thought about Colt, the door opened behind her. A large, dark figure entered the room.

"Dakota?" Colt called out to her.

"Over here." She breathed a sigh of relief.

He joined her by the window. "Are you okay? Did you get what you came for?"

"Yes. I'm sorry about earlier. I almost really messed things up."

"Don't worry about it. I understand." She took solace in his comforting tone.

"Thank you so much for helping me. I know you got what you came for, too. The duchess will be thrilled to get the Wingate collection back."

"Yeah. It went well, all things considered. Surprisingly well, which worries me. Mateo wasn't as volatile as I would have expected, and I can't figure out why."

"I agree. I know his temper, and being caught red-handed with the collection is kind of hard to dismiss in the eyes of the law. I even heard him laugh. It was eerie. You and Jack were amazing. It's obvious you two have worked together for quite a while, but I don't know how you can do it—face the danger, that is."

"It's not always easy and not always pretty, but knowing it makes a difference helps. Besides, somebody's got to do it. We need to get a move on. Let me see what you got so I can match it with the photos filed in the police report. Then we need to get you out of here. Jack's waiting down below."

"Yeah, I saw him. I finally understand where you're coming from, by the way. I realized when

I saw you and Jack with the cash and jewels. That's a lot of money and a lot of temptation. I get why you can't trust me completely."

"Thanks for understanding." His thumb grazed her cheek, the two of them close. She sensed he wanted to kiss her. Maybe it was the adrenaline racing through her body from the excitement of tonight, but the idea of him kissing her seemed perfect.

She was disappointed when he dropped his hand and looked down at the box in her hands.

Message received. All business, no pleasure. She opened the box and held her mother's jewelry for his inspection. The moonlight flooding through the window was just enough for him to see.

"Looks like a match to me. I'm glad you were telling the truth. Now we've got to get you out of here. You're free to leave after Jack drops you off at my place. I put the key to the house and your car keys under the cushion of the chair on the back porch. I need to stick around and wrap things up here." So, this was meant to be his nice to know you, but goodbye?

"But I thought—" She'd expected more from him.

"No. I'm not going with you. It's better this way, and I have a lot to do down at the station to work this out with the local law enforcement." He leaned his head down and dropped a kiss on her lips. "If you're not opposed, I'd still like to have our date before I have to head back to L.A."

Dakota smiled, still a little bewildered by his tender kiss. He wanted to see her again. Her heart leapt for joy while her mouth echoed the words. "I'd love to fix you dinner. Just say the word. Oh, wait, but on one condition."

"What is it with you and conditions? What is it this time?" he asked teasingly.

"Can I see the Wingate collection before you take them away and they get put under lock and key. Please," she begged. "They are almost never worn in public, and it would kill me to know I was this close and didn't get the chance to see them. Please." She touched his arm, hoping to keep him from turning her down and leaving.

"But it's dark in here, and we can't turn on the light." Colt didn't like her idea, but she recognized the weakness in his answer.

"We can go in the bathroom. There's no window, and we can flip on the light." She stretched up to land a kiss on his cheek. "Come on, it's just for a second."

"Fine. I know from experience you won't quit until you get your way." His tone hinted at a smile, proof he wasn't immune to her.

"Thanks. I promise I'll be quick."

They entered the bathroom, and Colt closed the door behind them before flipping on the light. He pulled the black box from his jacket pocket and placed it on the counter. "Have at it, princess—but no fingerprints."

Dakota pulled on a pair of plastic gloves from her backpack and then removed the top of the box slowly, savoring the moment. This was a once-in-a-lifetime opportunity. She took a deep breath, awestruck by the beauty of the Wingate necklace.

Perfectly matched ruby stones called to every fiber of her being, the need to look closer and savor the very essence of each beautiful, hand-cut gem undeniable. Crafted for the Queen of Portugal, the choker-style necklace was designed for Queen Amelia by her loving husband shortly before his death. The necklace had only made its way to the States after Queen Amelia's granddaughter inherited them, and she'd visited New York to attend her daughter's marriage to a senator.

Each teardrop stone was surrounded by small diamonds and placed one after the other to hang from the solid gold chain intricately braided and designed to draw maximum attention with its stunning display of craftsmanship.

Dakota pulled the jewelry kit from the side pocket of her backpack where she kept it stashed. Using the small soft-tipped tweezers, she picked up one of the earrings and held it up to the clear vanity lights above the mirror. The depth of color in the blood-red ruby appeared perfect.

After replacing the earring, she picked up the box, wanting to bring the necklace closer to the light. "Look at this." Using the tweezers, she picked up one of the teardrops to allow the light to pass through, letting Colt get a good look.

"They are very beautiful, but not as beautiful as you are when you smile. It was worth the risk to let you get a look at them just to see your reaction." Heat suffused her face, his compliment catching her off guard. And indeed, he was looking at her and not the most gorgeous necklace she'd ever laid eyes on.

She laid the teardrop back down on the cushioned velvet and picked up the brooch to examine it.

Colt touched a switch at his ear. "Yes. We're coming. Everything's fine."

He looked back at her, "You need to finish up. Jack's waiting, and we need to get you out of here."

"One last look, I promise."

Colt shuffled his feet impatiently but didn't answer.

Dakota put the brooch back in place and reached for the specialized loupe she kept in the kit. It was an expensive piece of equipment but worth every penny, the magnification level one of the highest possible. She picked up the earring again, holding it by the gold ball this time to let the light shine through better, and inspected it through the eyepiece. She wanted to experience the color and clarity she'd read about and had researched for hours and hours as part of her dissertation for graduation.

The brilliance fell short of her expectations. She looked again. Something wasn't quite right. Frowning, she changed the earring out for the other one. The result didn't change. To the naked eye, the piece was perfection, but to a trained eye with the loupe, and to someone who truly understood the heart of the ruby, it wasn't real.

"We need to go, Dakota."

"Wait. Something's wrong." She picked up the box, bringing the necklace closer to light, determined to look at each teardrop.

"What is it?" Colt asked. She could hear the worry in his voice, and rightly so. These stones were reproductions, good ones, but still not genuine. Victor had been trying to scam Antonio.

"I think they're fakes. Actually, I'm quite positive they aren't real."

"That's not possible. And we have five million dollars in cash to prove otherwise." The agitation in Colt's voice didn't bode well, but she couldn't change the truth.

Dakota shrugged. "Don't say I didn't tell you." She'd grown up in the jewelry business, training under father and then her uncle from the time she turned seven. She had learned and worked with some of the best gemologists in the world.

"It's time to go. I'm sure someone at headquarters will figure out whether you're right or not, but it may take some time to get someone experienced. Until then, Victor stays locked up. Let's just hope you're wrong, for both our sakes."

Colt was gone before she had a chance to ask him to explain. She was willing to risk her reputation on the fact they were fakes, and it hurt he hadn't trusted her assessment. Colt treated her like an amateur, but he'd find out the truth soon enough.

Chapter Ten

♥

JACK HELPED DAKOTA DOWN off the trellis and led her to the van. Neither one of them said a word. He opened the front passenger door, and she climbed inside, ready to get out of there. She clutched her backpack to her chest, knowing what it carried. "Phew. I'm glad that's over." She let out a deep breath to calm the fast rhythm of her heart.

"Me, too. Did you get what you were after?" Jack had turned to face her, asking the nonchalant question as he started the engine. She wasn't sure how to answer. He obviously knew the truth, whether Colt wanted him to or not.

He was the man's partner and trusted him with his life. And he was Colt's friend. "Yes." It was a simple answer and didn't reveal a thing.

"Thought so. Good." He nodded, put the van in drive, and pulled away from the curb.

Conversation shifted to small talk. Dakota determined to steer clear of the Wingate collection and her discovery. Colt could explain it to Jack in his own way and in his own time. It was of no concern to her. It still rankled Colt didn't trust her expertise.

Jack pulled into Colt's driveway. The house was dark, but she knew Halo was inside waiting for her. "Thanks for the ride. Hope I wasn't too much trouble." Dakota smiled as she opened the door, the light coming on overhead.

"You were fine. No worries. You know, Colt's a good guy. He may come across a little gruff at times, but he's got his reasons. And for the record, I never thought you were dating Mateo. I think Colt is a little off focus because he's attracted to you. Something I've not seen happen in a long time."

Jack was a good friend to Colt, probably knew him better than most, so hearing his words was nice. More than nice. At least until she remembered Colt's dismissal of her opinion tonight. "Thanks for believing in me *and* telling me. But there's more to this than you know, things I can't ignore. I'm sure he'll get around to telling you."

Jack leaned across the passenger seat and cast her an all-knowing look. "Give the guy a chance, you might be surprised."

"You forget, the guy has to want a chance. Colt's not into relationships, he told me so himself." *On several occasions.*

Jack looked surprised. "If he told you all that, you've had far more impact on him than you think."

"No. We agreed to have dinner before he leaves, but it's just that—dinner. My way to thank him for...everything." And now, she wasn't even sure she wanted to have dinner. Not after tonight.

"If that's what you think, you're not as smart as you look."

"Thanks a lot." She laughed, closing the door to end the conversation. Dakota waved and headed for the back of the house, the motion-detector flood light snapping on to light up the walkway.

Halo greeted her, yapping and nudging her hand as she entered through the back door and flipped on the light. She reached down to pet him, needing his comfort. It had been a long night, but it was over. She grabbed Halo's leash and his bag of food and headed for the garage. "Come on, boy. Let's go home." He jumped across her seat when she opened the driver-side door, eager to go for a ride.

Dakota pressed the button to open the automatic door and then slid in the driver's seat, tucking her backpack under the front seat. She wouldn't let it out of her sight, not after all she'd been through to get the jewelry back. She backed out of the driveway and headed for home.

Arriving back at her aunt and uncle's, they were happy to see her again. The small talk was driving her crazy, because she longed to lock herself in her room and inspect her mother's jewelry. All the way to the house, she tried to plan what she would say. She'd decided not to mention what she'd done.

When the time was right, she would, but for now, the fewer people who knew what she'd done, the better. And she was certain Colt and Jack wouldn't be spreading the word. She was relieved when her aunt and uncle went back to watching TV, leaving her to retire to her office.

Halo curled up at her feet, content to nap. Dakota pulled the box from her backpack. There was nothing to connect her to the disappearance of her mother's jewelry from Victor's, but he would know to where to look first because she'd caught him looking at the locket. It was another reason not to tell her aunt and uncle just yet. Luckily, Victor was in jail, which meant he wouldn't know they were even missing, at least for a little while.

But to be on the safe side, Dakota planned to keep their existence quiet, at least until Colt had a chance to relook at the accident records for her parents' car crash. It would take more than a burglary charge to keep Victor in prison for very long. It would take a murder charge.

Dakota pulled the pictures of her mother from the top drawer of her desk and then lined them up in a row at the top. As a gemologist, she was curious about the pieces she remembered her mother wearing. As a daughter who'd lost her parents, she was searching for an emotional connection that transcended between heaven and earth, hoping for peace in her heart.

A deep-seated sense of calm came over her as she lifted each piece out of the box, one by one. She was holding her mother's most prize possessions. Gifts from her father that showed his love in each intricately designed piece he'd molded for her. It had been a love that made her mother undeniably happy, and a love Dakota hoped to find one day.

She laid each piece down on the black velvet cloth tray she kept on her desk, awestruck by the beautiful craftmanship. Picking up her mother's locket, she held it lovingly in her hands. Dakota's eyes misted over as memories flooded her.

Laughing, singing, dancing. They'd all been happy together until the night of the accident.

Her mother kept tiny pictures of her and her father inside the locket, telling Dakota it was to keep him close to her heart, where he belonged. Dakota opened the heart-shaped locket and discovered the photo of her father missing. It must have slipped out.

An image of Victor dangling the locket and staring at it, an odd look on his face, came to mind. Colt's words echoed in her head, words she'd rejected at the time. *Victor and her mother had dated in high school.* If Colt was right, it would add the angle she'd been missing. *Jealousy.* It would also explain the creepy looks she remembered witnessing from the stairway as she watched her parents and the guests at their house parties. And it would explain why Victor had never sold off the collection.

Dakota's hands trembled as she picked up her loupe to inspect the locket closer. It sickened her to think of her mother with Victor, even if it was only dating in high school. At least she'd smartened up and married the right man. Dakota's father had been wonderful, the best father a daughter could ask for.

The locket wasn't fancy by any means. If anything, it was amateurish in design. It must have one of her father's earliest creations. Her mother had lots of gorgeous pieces, but this had been her favorite.

Dakota picked up her mother's most stunning piece next. It was the necklace she usually chose for the fanciest of the parties they attended. A princess cut stone, the aquamarine appeared to be almost four carats, its numerous facets designed to catch the light to reflect the medium-blue color. The stone was surrounded by fifteen quarter-carat diamonds, and the whole piece was set in eighteen-carat gold. The stones didn't strike her as high quality, the clarity not what she would have expected.

She picked up her cleaning cloth to polish the stones. Holding the loupe to her eye again, she re-inspected the piece, but nothing changed. The stones were real, but not the quality she would have expected her father to give her mother. The aqua was lighter in color and sported several inclusions deep within the gem. The lighter stone was not nearly as valuable as many of the ones she'd seen used for finely crafted artisan jewelry. And the diamonds were hardly worth including on the piece, more rough-cut chips. It didn't make sense.

Her father and her uncle had partnered together and created Decadence, a premier jewelry retailer selling some of the country's finest artisan jewelry. Everything in the store was top notch, individually designed, and personally inspected to ensure the gems were of the highest quality. So why was her mother's most impressive piece of jewelry not in the same league as what they sold at Decadence?

She picked up the photograph of her mother to compare the two pieces. There was no doubt it was the same piece—unless Victor had it replicated. But then with the Wingate jewels, they had used fakes, not low-quality genuine gems.

Her mother had said the piece was valuable because it represented love. Dakota had often dreamed it was worth millions, and her mother was a fairy princess that her father loved very much. It didn't matter to her what the piece was worth, like her mother had said, its value was in the love. And now, Dakota finally understood what she meant. It was a love like that she dreamed of finding for herself one day. Someone like Colt, perhaps. Too bad he wasn't a relationship kind of guy.

The piece was still worth over five thousand dollars, but it certainly wasn't worth stealing, much less murdering someone over. Victor must have been desperate when he stole the jewelry.

Your mother and Victor were a couple.

Maybe she'd been wrong all these years to link the two horrible events, but as child, that's exactly what she'd done. Maybe all Victor had ever wanted was something that belonged to her mother to treasure.

Piece by piece, she inspected them all. Aquamarine earrings. A gold-braided chain. Diamond necklace. Diamond earrings. Two rings. A sapphire and diamond necklace. All pieces that looked simply elegant and boasted unique and delicate craftmanship, and yet every one of them, including the rings, were of low-quality stones. The entire collection couldn't have been worth more than twenty-five to thirty thousand.

And Victor had kept the entire assortment of her mother's jewelry together, which was even more remarkable. It was perhaps another piece of the puzzle that pointed to the crazy idea he'd been in love with her mother. Jealousy made people do stupid things.

But why steal her jewelry knowing it would hurt her? It's not as if he would have known she would die that night. Or maybe that's why he kept everything. *Because she did die.*

Dakota was exhausted, and it was time to call it a night. She was starting to let her imagination run crazy. Tomorrow, she would look at everything again with a fresh eye and better lighting. And she wanted to see the police report.

She was curious what her aunt and uncle had listed as the value of the collection. Colt had asked her the question, but she hadn't known the answer. If her aunt and uncle had collected insurance against the loss, they would know the true value, or at least a very good estimate. It would be interesting to compare the two numbers.

She wasn't implying any wrongdoing on the part of her aunt and uncle, only whether everyone knew the value of the collection before it was stolen.

Chapter Eleven

♥

DAKOTA WOKE FEELING MORE tired than when she'd gone to sleep, if that were possible. Nightmares had come and gone, along with visions of Victor coming after her. Her mind was playing tricks, remembering the past. Halo slept next to her and must have sensed her unease, because he was glued to her side.

He looked up at her as she slid out bed. "Good morning, Halo. Sorry if I kept you awake last night." She leaned over and gave him a good head scratching, followed by a pat on the back. He lay back down when she went in the bathroom. They had a routine, although this morning, it was a little later than normal.

After she got dressed, Halo followed her to the kitchen. Her aunt and uncle were early risers and always left her a couple of cups of coffee in the pot. One to chase away the cobwebs from the night, the other to take Halo out to potty and for a morning walk.

This morning, a third might be in order, but then the caffeine would leave her agitated. Better to stay away from number three, especially with everything she needed to accomplish today.

She poured herself a cup and flipped on the TV to watch Good Morning Gold Coast. Dash Diamond was the star of the show, but it was the mascot, Star, who stole the hearts of everyone who watched. And of course, Halo watched the show with her every morning because Star was his sister. Dakota was sure he recognized her. They looked similar, except Star's coloring was a little lighter than Halo's reddish tones.

She hadn't taken but a few sips of coffee when the name Victor Mateo splashed across the screen at the bottom. Dakota turned up the

TV to hear the report. It gave her a sense of satisfaction to know it had all been real and that Victor was locked up.

Dakota grabbed Halo's leash and headed outside. She took him down the street to the dog park and let him run. He hadn't had much exercise the past few days, and it would be good for him.

Thirty minutes later, they were back home and settled. Halo was worn out from playing and jumped on her bed, and curled up, sleep clearly a priority. Dakota laughed and headed for her office. After opening the blinds to let in more natural light, she sat down at her desk and pulled the box back out from the top drawer. Piece by piece, she re-inspected the jewelry. Nothing changed. The collection was good, but not what she'd imagined as a child.

She straightened, her back stiff from being bent over for such a long time. Extending her arms over her head, she tried to stretch away the ache in her shoulders and neck, and then rolled her shoulders in circles to loosen the muscles.

Dakota closed her eyes briefly, letting her head come to rest in the palm of her hand, her elbows braced against the surface of the desk. Lost deep in concentration, it took her a second to register a sound from behind her.

A tingle shot up her spine.

She opened her eyes and turned to see what made the sound.

Victor. And a gun.

Dakota screamed. Victor holding a gun transported back to a time when she was twelve. It was dark again. Terror took hold, her body shaking. "Halo," she called, her voice not sounding like her own. He was her lifeline. Where was he? She couldn't breathe.

Victor moved closer. "Shut up. There's no one here to save you, and your stupid dog is locked in your room," he snarled.

"Halo," Dakota whimpered. She wanted to cry but couldn't. She wanted to run, but she was trapped. She wanted Colt to protect her, but he wasn't here. She was on her own, just like last time.

She started to rock back and forth. "What do you want? Why are you here?" She tried to use her body to shield her mother's jewelry from his view.

He knew. It was the only explanation. She was completely at Victor's mercy.

"You know exactly why I'm here. Don't play stupid, it doesn't become you. I'm not sure how you managed this—" he waved the gun toward the jewelry, "—and you clearly didn't expect me this morning. The question is, why?" His face darkened in rage. "You know they arrested me, and you felt confident I was in jail." He shook his head. "Funny thing is, the law can't hold a man very long for trying to sell hand-crafted artisan fakes for a ton of money." His dry, merciless laugh sent shivers down her spine.

She'd known they were fakes, so Victor's confirmation came as no surprise. But it also meant the FBI knew and must have had to release Victor. It stung to realize Colt hadn't bothered to warn her.

But then, his protection had ended last night, and she was no longer his responsibility. Maybe he'd had second thoughts about getting together once this was over. Whatever his reasoning, she'd been left to face Victor alone. And she was smart enough to know this wouldn't end well.

Halo was barking like crazy just down the hall. Too bad Dakota hadn't taught him how to open doors. "I don't know what you're talking about." The only chance she had was to keep playing dumb. *And pray.*

"You're a liar. Your mother's jewelry wasn't the only box in the safe, and yet the other box was left untouched. Only you would be so noble. And until last night, that collection you're admiring was in my possession. I want to know how you got it." He advanced closer; his gun trained on her.

She swallowed hard. "I saw you with my mother's locket and wanted it back. It was a surprise to find the rest of her jewelry with it." She stood, trying to reason with him.

"Don't lie to me! Box it up. And no sudden moves. You and I need to take a little ride."

Trying to reason with a madman was impossible, and there was no way she wanted to go anywhere with him. She turned back to the table slowly. Her hands shook as she tried to collect the pieces and put them in the box. Dakota glanced around the desk, but there was nothing close by that she could use to defend herself, especially against a gun.

Her gaze strayed to her phone. She carefully edged one hand toward her phone and pressed the button to open the camera and then hit record.

"What do you want with my mother's jewelry? You and I both know it's not very valuable," she said, her voice calmer than she could have thought possible under the circumstances. It was somewhat reassuring to know everything they said was being recorded.

"Value is not always monetary. Hurry it up. We haven't got all day," he ordered.

She glanced back at him. "Did you like my mother?" Dakota had nothing to lose by asking such a bold question, and everything to gain. She wanted the truth.

Victor seemed startled. He raised his hand and rubbed his forehead as if in pain.

Dakota took advantage of the moment to slide a piece of the black velvet across the face of the phone to hide it. If Victor forced her to go with him, at least everyone would know who'd taken her and where to begin looking.

"What are doing?" he snapped.

She let her hand stray to the pile of photos she had on her desk. The photos of her mother. "I'm getting one of my favorite pictures of my mother to show you. You seem to be interested in her belongings." Dakota held it out to him.

"A picture of Chloe?" His eyes darkened fiercely, but he didn't move to take it from her. "If that's what those are, I want all of them."

And there it was. Victor had been in love with her mother and still loved her to this day. "So, I'm guessing you *liked* her a lot?"

"Liked? I loved her. And she left me for the no-body you call your father. You're a lot like him. Foolish. Nobody takes what's mine and lives to tell about it." Raw pain gripped each word he uttered. It was like watching a scene out of a terrifying movie, but one she couldn't hit the power button to end the nightmare.

"What's that supposed to mean?" Crazy thoughts rushed through her head, none of them good. Had she been right all along? She had to keep him talking. Show him the pictures. Stall. Maybe her aunt and uncle would come home. Wishful thinking. They never came home during the day.

"Your father stole the love of my life, and you stole my jewels. There's a price for such treach-ery." The veins across Victor's forehead popped out like they were about to explode, his face red and contorted with rage.

Dakota knew her only chance against him was to keep calm and wait for an opportuni-ty against this madman. The sound of Halo barking and scratching at the bedroom door strengthened her resolve. She was older and stronger than she had been all those years ago, and she had to prevail for Halo. She needed to prove to her faithful friend his years of support hadn't been for naught.

"But they weren't your jewels. They were my mother's, and therefore rightfully mine. I took back what belonged to me in the first place."

His eyes glazed over. "They're all I have left of her. Chloe got mad and broke it off with me, but she always came back because she loved me. But the last time it happened, your father got in the way. When he gave her that cheap locket, she thought she loved him and never came back to me." It was as though he was in his own world—remembering.

"What's so special about the locket?" she had to ask, had to keep him talking. Victor was the enemy, but he was the man with the answers she'd longed to know for years.

"He made it for her. Cheap gold. Just look at it," he snarled. "It's nothing. I gave her a diamond necklace, and she never liked to wear it. But a simple handmade gold bauble on a chain tricked her into thinking she loved him. Finish up! We need to leave," he snapped, taking another menacing step toward her.

Her hands trembled as she put the last of the jewelry back into the box. Dakota refused to believe him. Her mother had loved her father more than anything else, and every day she'd been a witness to that love. Victor was wrong. "But you were all friends. You were at our house, our parties. I remember." She dared to look up at him to see his reaction.

"I always hoped she'd get bored and leave your father. But she never did. She was too weak to leave him on her own, and I grew tired of waiting. I took matters into my own hands, knowing she'd come back to me if he was out the picture." The implication of his words sank in.

Victor had wanted her father dead. But if he wanted her mother back, why did he kill her also? Her stomach lurched, and she fought back the wave of nausea threatening to consume her as she realized she was standing face-to-face with her parents' killer.

Fighting back the numb feeling, she pushed for more truth, knowing they were being recorded. No matter what happened to her, the world would know what happened that night. Colt would make sure of it.

She chose her words with care. "But they both died in the accident. How could she come back to you?"

"She wasn't supposed to be in the car. She was at the opera. I gave her the tickets. I saw her leave with her friend. I would give anything to have her back. But I can't. Just like I can't change what I need to do now. It's a shame you had to get in the way. More the pity I must kill you, too. Let's go."

Dakota's legs were like jelly, her body shaking. But with a gun pointed at her, there was little she could do except follow his orders and hope for a miracle.

Like Colt.

Victor snatched the box from her hand when she drew close, forcing her out the door ahead of him. They walked down the hall, the gun digging into the small of her back.

"You have the jewels, why not let me go?" she tried to reason with the maniac.

"Because you're too much like your father. I'd hoped you would be more like your mother. I wanted to pretend you were the daughter we never had. You're a miniature copy of your mother, but I've discovered you're not her. No one can ever be her."

Chapter Twelve

♥

COLT COULD COUNT ON one hand the hours of sleep he'd gotten the night before. Three to be precise. After he'd processed the initial paperwork for Victor's arrest, he'd turned his efforts to digging deeper into the two Mitchell cases. Yes, he'd promised Dakota, but it wasn't for that reason alone that he'd given up a good night's rest.

There were just enough discrepancies in the files, that as an investigator, his gut was telling him there was more to the coincidence of the two events happening the same night. Dakota had proven Victor had possession of the stolen family jewelry, and Mateo's prior relationship with Chloe Mitchell was more than enough reason to reopen the investigation.

Possession of stolen merchandise didn't necessarily make Victor the culprit, but with his known preclusion as a jewelry thief, it certainly made him the prime suspect, and Dakota's testimony could no longer be ignored. It was too bad there was no mention of a tattoo on the report. Even the mention of one would have been helpful in order to bring charges.

Colt believed Dakota and her recollection of what happened that fateful night, but it would take more than his belief in her testimony to get a conviction—or even his commander's go-ahead to issue a warrant.

It was odd the two files had never been linked. There wasn't any evidence of cross-reference to the events. Which either meant poor work ethic by the officer in charge of the case, or money changed hands to make the situation go away. Either way, the signs pointed to a definite problem, and neither officer still worked at the

RCPD. Both had been discharged within six months of the accident for conduct issues.

Talking to the officers currently employed at RC headquarters would be like trying to break into Fort Knox. The words *off the record* came to mind.

The shrill ring of Jack's ringtone blared from the across the room. Jack was one of the few callers he never ignored. He retrieved his phone and hit the connect button. "Morning. What's up that you're calling me this early?"

"We've got a problem. A big, big problem," Jack said, the tone of his voice not one of Colt's favorites. Trouble was on the horizon.

"Shoot."

"Victor's out." Colt was instantly alert, the two words spurring him into a fully alert mode.

"What are you talking about? I barely got the reports filed before midnight, and it's like eight in the morning. Why would they let him out?" Colt shook his head. This wasn't good.

"The jewels he was selling last night were fake. The RCPD won't process charges against him because there's no law against selling hand-crafted custom jewelry for a lot of dough. He was out at first light and taken home."

Dakota. She'd been right about them being fakes. He should have paid more attention and not chalked her words up to an inexperienced eye. If Mateo discovered the Mitchell collection missing, she was in trouble.

"Dakota's not safe. Someone should have told us about this before it happened." Colt grabbed his keys and headed for the garage.

"Are you finally going to tell me what you let her take? 'Cause it looks like this is going to get ugly, and I need to know what we're dealing with."

"It was her family's jewelry collection. I've been looking through the files of the accident the night her parents died thirteen years ago. The same night their home was broken into. My suspicions lead me to believe the two cases are connected." He started the car and backed out, his tires squealing against the cement.

"Wow. I'm sure you had your reasons, but this isn't good. Why would Mateo still have the jewelry? He doesn't keep stuff lying around."

"This was personal, not business." And it was about to get more personal. Colt had to get to Dakota and protect her.

"Then you need to find Dakota. Mateo's not one to mess with."

"I know. I'm already out the door and headed to her place as we speak." He'd have someone's head for this royal screw up, but right now, his priority was keeping her safe. "Stay close to your phone, and I'll keep you posted."

"Will do."

Colt knew time was critical. The minute Victor discovered Chloe Mitchell's jewelry missing, he'd head straight for Dakota, knowing she'd seen the locket and would be his prime suspect. There was no telling what Victor would do to her, but one thing was for certain, it wouldn't be pretty. Mateo didn't play around.

He dialed Dakota's number, praying she'd answer. It rang and rang, but she didn't answer.

Her voice mail kicked on. Leaving a message wasn't his first choice, but it would have to do until he got to her place.

"Hey there. Hate to have to give you bad news, but Mateo is out on a technicality. A rather large one. Turns out you were right. The jewels were fake. If he discovers your mother's jewelry missing, he might come after you. Call me ASAP. I'm worried about you."

Colt hung up the phone and stepped on the gas. He blew his horn as he went through a red light, intent on getting to where she lived. Minutes later, he pulled in the driveway. The first thing he noticed was that her car was missing, which meant she wasn't home since she never let anyone else drive it.

He knocked on the front door anyway, just to be thorough. Colt waited, hoping someone would answer. Halo barked from somewhere inside—the sound coming from the upstairs area. Without giving it much thought, he tried the door, happy to find it unlocked.

"Dakota? Anyone here?"

No one answered, but Halo's barking grew more frantic. It sounded like the dog was trying to bust down the door with all the racket he was making.

Colt shoved aside his fear of dogs and headed up the stairs, determined to get to Halo and search for answers. He pushed open the door to find Halo growling at him, teeth barred. "Easy, boy. It's me." The memory of another time, another dog flashed before his eyes. Colt broke out in a cold sweat.

Almost instantly, Halo went quiet. He approached Colt and nudged his hand to let him know it would be okay. Colt patted his head. "Good boy."

Halo barked.

"Where's Dakota, boy? Is she here? Can you show me where she's at?"

Halo took off down the hall and went into her office to look around, Colt following close on his heels. The dog looked around and sniffed. He let out a low growl, searching the room and then following the scent back down the stairs and to the back door of the house. Colt stayed close, hoping Halo would lead him to Dakota.

They went around the side of the house and stopped in the driveway, where Halo sat. He'd lost the scent right where Dakota parked her car. Maybe he was flipping out for nothing. Maybe she'd simply gone to the store, and Halo was unhappy at being left behind.

Either way, Colt had to find her, and he wouldn't stop worrying until he did. Colt headed back in the house and grabbed Halo's leash off the hook on the wall. "Come on, boy. Let's go find her." The dog raced ahead to his car like he understood. Colt opened the front passenger door, and the dog jump in. He lowered the back of the seat to make it easier for him to lie down.

Halo nudged his hand by way of thanks, or maybe like before, he sought to comfort him. Colt called Jack to update him. "She's not at the house. Halo was there and acting all crazy. I've got him with me but have no idea where to look."

"Have you thought about checking Decadence? Or even back at your place. Maybe she went to see you. It's obvious you two have something going on between you."

"You know I don't mix business with pleasure. Let's stay focused." Colt drove toward Decadence.

"Whatever you say."

Colt slowed to go through the intersection, ignoring the stop sign but being cautious. "Wait, did you ever take her bracelet off?"

"No, sorry. Oh, wow, not sorry. Pull her up on the tracker app and let me know what I can do to help, 'cause if you're this worried, I am too. You've got a sixth sense about these things that's never good."

"Will do." Colt hung up the phone and flipped open the computer attached by a retractable arm to the dash. He pulled over to the side of the road, typed in a few details, and then waited for the screen to populate. There was still hope she was out running errands or at the store like Jack suggested, but Colt wasn't taking any chances.

Halo sat up, watching with interest. Smartest dog he'd ever met.

The tracker picked up on Dakota's location. The beeper showed her headed out of town. *Where was she going and why*? A sense of deep dread ripped through him, and Halo nudged his hand again. "Thanks, boy. You want me to stay calm and focused. I get it."

Colt called Jack again. "Dakota's headed out of town, and I'm going after her. I've got to make sure she's okay, or at least warn her, and she's not answering her phone."

"Any chance she's on the run with Mateo?"

"Not a chance. Come on, Jack. You've met her. She doesn't have a diabolical bone in her body."

"I wouldn't know, but I do trust you. You've always been a good judge of character. What can I do?"

"I'm headed out of town on Route 17. Right now, she's about two miles out of Redwood Cove city limits. Head that way, and I'll let you know if I find out anything else."

"Roger that."

They both knew Colt's track record detecting when something was wrong was highly predictable. Close to ninety percent. And ninety percent was ninety percent too much when it came to Dakota and her safety.

Exactly the reason he'd sworn off relationships. His job was dangerous. It was his fault she had taken back the jewelry. And if he'd been on top of things, he'd have known about Victor's release. It would have given him time to get to Dakota and put her in protective custody until they were able to get Victor on solid charges.

He tried her phone again, but there was still no answer.

Colt raced through town in the direction Dakota had taken. Glancing over at the laptop, he kept checking the tracker and her progress. She was driving slowly, which was to his advantage.

Even if everything was fine, when she got his voicemail, it would toss her into a sea of turmoil, and any peace she'd found over the years would be shattered. Colt pressed the gas pedal deeper to the floor. She was still headed out of town, but he was determined to catch up with her.

He drove through red lights and stop signs, disregarding the angry glares and horns and an occasional middle finger from some of the townspeople and tourists.

It was pure luck Jack hadn't removed the bracelet. There was no doubt he'd find her. He just hoped it would be in time. Once she was back under Colt's protection, Mateo wouldn't get near her.

Halo sat up, leaning his body against the passenger door and looking out the window. Colt patted the dog when it was safe to do so, as much for the dog's benefit as his own.

Closing the distance between him and the flashing icon on the screen, he slowed to get a better read on her location. The flashing icon turned red to indicate she'd stopped. There were only a couple of seaside vista points overlooking the steep cliffs that bordered the sea on this section of the road.

Colt slowed, expecting her to cross paths with him soon. He watched for the bright blue of her Mustang. *Not much farther now.* The beep on his computer alerted him Dakota was on the move again, the icon turning green and headed in his direction. Good. She was headed back to town.

There. Just ahead, he could see her car coming his way. He stopped, flashed his lights, and then rolled his window down, signaling for her to pull over. Colt let out a huge sigh of relief.

Halo barked, as if sensing the change in him. The dog caught sight of her car and started dancing excitedly. As Dakota's vehicle drew almost level with his, he realized she wasn't slowing or making any attempt to stop. Worse still, she wasn't driving the car.

No one was.

Something was desperately wrong. The flashing icon passed him, and the car kept going. Colt looked back over his shoulder, stunned.

The cliff. She was headed straight for the cliff, and if the car didn't turn, she'd go over.

"Hang on, boy." Colt braced the dog with one hand, accelerated, and turned the wheel sharply, spinning the car one hundred and eighty degrees, the tires squealing in protest. Pedal to the floor, he raced ahead of the Mustang and zipped out passed her on the left, grateful there was no oncoming traffic.

As he passed her car, there was still no sign of Dakota, and the sharp curve was just ahead. Adrenaline shot through him, his emotions in overdrive. He would only get one chance to get this right. He dragged Halo across his lap, locking one arm around him. It was harder to maneuver the car, but it was the only way he knew to protect the dog on impact.

Colt pulled ahead of the Mustang and turned sharply to the right, slamming on his brakes. Her car smashed headlong into the side of his, metal on metal, the sound deafening. The force of the impact drove Colt into the driver's door, the airbag exploding in his face as everything came to a stop. Momentarily stunned, he tried to get his bearings.

Halo struggled against him.

Colt relaxed his death grip on the dog. "You okay, boy?"

Halo licked his face.

"Guess that's a yes." Colt rubbed his head to help shake off the fog. Nothing wrong with him a few pain killers wouldn't help.

Dakota. He needed to get to Dakota.

He struggled to move the safety air bag out of the way, a task made more difficult by Halo. Colt pushed open the door and slid out, Halo close behind him. The dog ran ahead toward the Mustang. Colt stepped out the car, stumbling at first, and then following at a much slower pace, his legs taking a little while longer to recover from the jolt.

The engine of the Mustang was smoking, the front end squashed against his car. Halo jumped at the driver-side door and barked. "Down, boy." The dog sat and waited for him. Colt was stunned to discover Dakota in the driver's seat slumped against the dash and unconscious.

Halo tried to push past him to get to Dakota.

"Stay," Colt commanded, surprised when the dog listened.

He leaned in and felt for a pulse, relieved to feel the erratic but definite beat of her heart.

"Dakota. Can you hear me? Come on, sweetheart, open your eyes." He didn't want to move her until he knew it was safe, but it was next to impossible not to pull her into his arms and hold her close. "Dakota, come on. I'm right here and not going anywhere."

Colt had to help her, but he felt helpless, not knowing what was wrong. Reaching for his phone he hit redial. "I found her. Get an ambulance up here. Route 17 about ten miles out of town. She's unconscious, and I've wrecked her car. I'm afraid to move her until she comes to."

"Got it. I'm on my way. Hang in there, Colt."

Chapter Thirteen

♥

A DEEP GROAN SLID from Dakota's throat, the pain in her head unbearable.

"Dakota, sweetheart, can you hear me?" Colt's voice called to her, bringing her back from the hazy, dark depths.

She tried to speak, wetting her lips first. They were so dry. And nasty. Dakota dragged the back of her hand against her mouth, trying to get rid of the foul taste. "Colt."

"I'm right here, Dakota. The ambulance is on its way. You've been in an accident. I'm sorry about your car, but there was nothing else I could do." *Accident. Her car. What was he talking about?*

"Victor." She had to tell Colt what had happened. If only her head would quit hurting. She tried to move, but a pain shot up her leg, forcing her to hold still. A deep throbbing pulsated from her ankle area.

"What about Victor?" Colt's voice was urgent.

"Victor did this." She tried not to think of the pain, needing to get the words out to tell Colt what happened.

"No. It was me. I crashed into you. I thought something was wrong and you were going to drive over the cliff. I'm sorry."

Colt tried to kill her. No. No. That wasn't right. She had to focus. Get him to understand. "Victor. Out of jail. Trying to kill me."

"Victor was with you? He's not here now. Let's get you taken care of, and then you can tell me about it."

She started to shake her head no, but the move only made her head hurt worse. "He put a rag over my mouth. Horrible taste. I don't remember anything after that." Dakota tried to push up with one arm. "Help me," she pleaded.

"I'm afraid to move you until the paramedics get here. Does anything hurt?" The concern in his voice was touching. She'd have to remember that later, after she killed him for not warning her Victor got out.

Halo whimpered.

"Halo?" She lifted her arm to make contact, needing him close, but her hand fell back. It was as if she had no energy. Halo nudged her hand, and she felt his warm tongue licking her fingers. Dakota took a deep breath and smiled, a sense of calmness filling her. *Colt and Halo were here.* Everything would be okay.

"It would be better if you didn't move until we make sure there are no internal injuries. Can you tell me if anything hurts?" he asked again.

"My head hurts like someone crashed a brick down on it, and there's pain radiating up my right leg when I try to move. Feels like my ankle." Dakota cradled her head, trying to ward off the pounding.

When the wave of nausea passed, she braced herself with one arm and tried to push up. "Help me, Colt. Please." She was determined to sit up and shake off the awful, drugged feeling still clouding her brain.

Colt helped her to an upright position in the driver's seat, his touch gentle. "How do you feel now? Better? Worse?" He sounded like a worried mother hen. The thought caused her to smile. Well, at least want to smile. She couldn't quite muster the action.

"No worse. Maybe a little better." Her words were coming stronger with each passing minute, and the ache in her head was subsiding. She wished she could say the same for ankle.

"I'm sure the ambulance will be here any minute. They can check you over and take you to the hospital for x-rays."

"I can't go anywhere until you know what happened." Dakota didn't know when she'd see Colt again, and the thought was upsetting. She continued to pet Halo, her strokes becoming stronger, more needy.

"Go ahead then and tell me if you're up to it." Colt looked down the road at the sound of sirens far off in the distance. "We don't have long."

"Victor paid me a visit this morning."

Colt closed his eyes, shook his head, and took a deep breath. "I tried to warn you he was out, but obviously I was too late."

"I wondered why you hadn't." It was nice to know Colt had tried and that he cared.

"I'm sorry. The Redwood Cove police didn't think to let me know. But then in all fairness, they didn't know what you and I knew about your mother's jewelry."

"Victor knows. I knew when he found out he'd come calling. I thought if I hid them and never let them surface, he'd eventually believe me and go away. But he caught me by surprise with the collection on my desk. He took them from me. Please don't let him get away with everything." Her voice broke, tears running down her face.

"Everything meaning what?"

"Murder. He killed my parents, and he just tried to k-kill me." Halo nudged her, the dog's whining becoming more frequent as her agitation increased. Dakota took several deep, calming breaths and then rubbed Halo's head, trying to reassure him.

"I believe you, but we need proof." Colt was tense, the lines across his forehead like deep ravines.

"I have it, thanks to you." This time, she smiled—really smiled—as pieces of what transpired came back to her.

"What do you mean?"

"The proof is on my phone. I remembered you recording our little chat the first time we talked. My phone was on the desk so when Victor wasn't paying attention, I pressed the button for the camera and then record. I captured most of the conversation, more than enough for evidence. Trust me." It had been a stroke of genius. Daring, but genius.

"That a girl. I can't believe the chances you took, but it all worked out." Colt shook his head. "I'm sorry about your parents. I know you've suspected as much since you found out Victor

was the one who stole your mother's jewelry."
Colt brushed her hair back from her face, and
then moved his hand to trail his thumb across
her cheek. Soft and gentle.

Dakota tried to move again but stopped short,
the pain in her ankle a bit much to bear. It felt
like the size of a balloon squished in her sneaker.
"Honestly, I started to think I was wrong. It's
hard knowing the truth, but at least my parents were together. They loved each other that
much," she said, tears running down her face
again.

"I'm sorry, sweetheart." Colt leaned in and
hugged her, the feel of his arms just as comforting as having Halo nearby. *More.*

She tried to shove the unhappy thoughts
aside. There would plenty of time to deal with
those when she was alone. "Victor told me
the jewels were fakes." She gave him her best
I-told-you-so smile, all while trying not to move
her leg at all, using her hands as braces.

"Yes, you were right. I was wrong. Guess I'll
know better in the future not to doubt you."

"The future?" She liked the sound of that.

"You know, the dinner you promised me when this is all over." He grinned.

She should have known he didn't mean anything else. He'd already been super clear about his no-relationship rule. But it didn't mean she couldn't tease him. "Careful, Colt, I might start to think you care about more than protecting me."

"Protecting you is my job." The gleam in his eyes gave her hope that perhaps it was more than that. The trick would be convincing him to act on his feelings.

"It's a date."

The ambulance wasn't far off by the sounds of it. Colt spotted Jack's car as it came screeching to a halt nearby. His partner jumped out of the car and came running toward them.

"How is she?" Jack spoke to Colt, but his gaze was directed on her.

"You could ask me, you know. I'm not comatose. And other than a slight headache and a throbbing leg, not to mention a destroyed car,

I'm doing good. Thanks for asking." Dakota shot Jack a smile.

"Nothing wrong her brain or her tongue, I see." Jack chuckled.

Colt shook his head. "By the sounds of it, she may have a sprained ankle. I didn't want to remove her shoe to help keep the swelling down until the paramedics arrived. Her headache seems to be letting up, which is a good sign. I still want the medical team to check her over and transport her to the Redwood Cove hospital for x-rays for both the ankle and the head to be on the safe side."

They were discussing her like she wasn't even there and had no say in the matter.

"I'm fine, thanks to Colt. Would you two *please* go after Victor. He's a murderer, and I want him to pay for destroying my family." The longer they stood here, the more distance Victor put between them, and the last thing she wanted was for him to escape.

"What's going on?" Jack asked.

"What's going on is that Victor tried to kill me, and he killed my parents. He can't have gotten too far, because he's on foot back that way." She pointed back up the road. "If you delay, he could get away." Dakota reached out to touch Colt, trying to make him understand the urgency.

Colt glanced sharply at her. "What do you mean? You didn't tell me this part."

"I've been trying to tell you. He forced me to drive here and then put a cloth over my mouth. After the foul taste, I don't remember anything until I woke up to the sound of you calling my name. But I did see him jump out of the car before everything went black."

"Chloroform." Colt said, shooting a look at Jack.

"He said the crash would look like an accident or suicide, and that considering it's the same cliff my parents went over, he figured they'd rule suicide. The man is sick, and he needs to be stopped."

The ambulance arrived and the paramedics headed their way.

"I'm glad you're mostly okay, Dakota. You sit tight, let them check you over, and we'll take care of finding Mateo. Don't you worry about a thing except getting better." Jack was trying to reassure her.

Jack and Colt stepped back. Colt grabbed Halo by the collar and gave him a tug. "Halo, come." The dog went with him without any resistance, surprising her.

"Listen, Jack. I know we're partners, but any chance you can handle this on your own with some of the local law enforcement? I'm not leaving Dakota. At least, not yet."

Dakota couldn't help but overhear the two guys talking as the paramedics moved in, bringing their medical bags. The fact Colt wanted to stay was more than a little sweet, but it wouldn't be right for him to leave his partner, not to mention, it was his job.

"I understand. I wouldn't want to leave my woman in this situation, either."

"She's not my woman. We're just friends." Colt uttered the words, confirming what Dakota already knew. Their future entailed being friends. Not exactly what she had in mind considering she'd started to fall for the big galoot.

"If you say so. I'll call for backup, and we'll have this area surrounded in no time." Jack shrugged and walked away to talk with some of the other new arrivals.

"Can you tell me what happened, ma`am?" The paramedic pulled out his blood pressure cuff and wrapped it around her around arm.

Dakota caught him up to speed as he checked her eyes, her pulse, and her blood pressure.

Halo started barking. She peered around the side of the paramedic trying to see what was happening. The dog was running back and forth between Jack and Colt. Dakota had never seen him act like that before.

Colt turned in her direction. "Hey, Dakota, what's wrong with Halo? He's gone nuts."

She watched as Halo grabbed Colt's hand in his mouth and tried to gently pull him toward

Jack. Colt pulled his hand out of reach, a look of concern etched across his features.

"No, Halo. Sit," she commanded, loud enough for him to hear and respond.

Colt shot her a look of gratitude.

"I need you to sit still while I check out your ankle, ma'am. I'm going to get your shoe off and get it wrapped in an ice pack before we try to move you. The cold should help reduce the pain a bit." The paramedic was trying his best, but she had other things on her mind, and he'd just have to wait a few seconds.

"I'm sorry. Just give me a minute." She looked up as Colt came to stand nearby, waiting for answers. "I'm not sure what he's doing. He's never done that before." Dakota shrugged. "I heard you talking to Jack. You don't need to stay with me. You're his partner, and he needs you. You've got a job to do, and I'm in good hands."

"No. I need to be here. With you. Which is where I should have been before Victor was released." Colt was feeling guilty for something that wasn't his fault.

"I keep telling you I'll be fine. You two are a team, and if anything happens to him, you'll never forgive me or yourself. Go," she ordered.

Colt looked to where Jack was talking with some of the officers who had joined in on the action. Halo had come to sit next to Colt.

"Looks like you made a friend."

Colt looked back at her, a huge grin on his face. "I reckon so. Must have been somewhere between the time he almost chewed off my arm and when he realized I wasn't Mateo. I'm just glad he figured it out in time."

Ouch. That didn't sound good at all—for Colt. "He's acting like he wants to go with you guys, which is weird. He would never leave my side voluntarily unless he thought there was a good reason." There was more to Colt's story, like the beginning, and she'd have to ask him about it sometime, but right now, the guys had a job to do.

"Hey, Colt. What's up with this crazy dog?" Jack crossed back to where Colt stood and gave

Halo a few good pats on the back and down his sides.

"Dakota thinks he wants to go with us."

"Us?" Jack asked, one eyebrow raised in question.

"She's pushing me to go with you."

"He needs to go. I'm not a baby, and these guys will take good care of me." She nodded to the paramedic working on her ankle.

"I'm staying out of that decision." Jack held up his hand and stepped back.

The pain had already started to subside with the ice pack, and going to the hospital was just a technicality. She fought back against reacting as the ace bandage was wrapped around her foot and ankle, not wanting to give Colt a reason to stay.

"I think I know what's up with Halo. Whenever I go out of town, I leave him with Logan and Hanna Moss. Logan is a park ranger who works with search and rescue dogs. Logan mentioned he'd been working with Halo when he stayed there. Maybe the police cruisers and uniformed officers have got him excited, and he thinks he's going on a search and rescue mission."

"More like a search and destroy mission. Halo's probably got it in for Victor after he locked him in your room."

Dakota smiled. "True. He went ballistic after I screamed. I could hear him scratching and jumping on the door to get out."

"I think this is his way to protect you, making sure Mateo doesn't slip away. And he got some good smells of Mateo from of your office when I let him out of the bedroom. Maybe he's picking up Mateo's scent."

"That's reasonable."

"You okay with him going? Could be helpful." Colt nodded, as if deciding for himself it was a good idea as well.

"I'm not a huge fan, but then I wish you didn't have to go either. But I understand it's for the best. Besides, I trust you."

Colt's gaze intensified, but he didn't answer her right away. She could almost see the wheels turning in his brain.

"Give me your sweater." Colt held out his hand.

"Why? That's a weird request."

"Mateo's been in the car with you, and his scent will be on it. It will keep the smell fresh for Halo."

"Great idea. Victor pushed me into the car and then wrapped his arms around my throat when he used the chloroform on me. His stink should be all over it. Here," she said, slipping out of her sweater and handing it to him.

"What are you thinking, Colt?"

"I'm thinking you have two extras along for the search, partner."

"Works for me. Tres amigos." Jack laughed.

"Friends with a dog? Me? Hardly." Colt shrugged. "Dakota said they pulled off into the Cliff Walk vista just up the road about a half mile. He didn't have a car, and there's only the sea on one side and woods on the others. We can fan out and check the woods." Colt turned back to her, leveling her with a hard gaze. "But I'm only going if you promise me that you'll go to the hospital for x-rays and you'll stay with your aunt and uncle until I get back."

"I promise." Dakota smiled, hoping to reassure him.

"And I'm assigning a security officer to stick with you until Mateo's been arrested."

"That's a bit extreme."

"My way, or I stay. Take your pick. I'm not taking any chances that Mateo circles back around and finds a way to get to you if he discovers you didn't go over the cliff. Your testimony makes you a walking target."

"Fine. Your way." The image Colt had painted left her a little nervous. Or a lot nervous. She'd be glad for the extra security, and maybe when this was over, she'd thank him.

"Jack, I'll get his leash and a few things out of my car, and then we can head out. Let the others know the change in plans. And get one of the other officers assigned as full-time security detail on Dakota. Wherever she goes, he goes, until Mateo is back behind bars. Make sure they are clear on the orders."

"Will do." Jack was quick to agree.

"Can I go to the bathroom alone?"

"Not even going to justify that question with an answer. Just be careful while I'm gone." Colt leaned down and dropped a kiss on her lips. "Take care and don't forget your promise."

Dakota raised her hand, letting her fingertips touch where his lips had. "I won't. And, Colt, stay safe—all of you." He raised a hand in farewell, turned, and walked away, Halo hot on his heels.

The paramedics wheeled a gurney up, which seemed totally ridiculous. If it hadn't been for her promise to Colt, she would have had a thing or two to say about the transportation. She also knew the guys were just doing their job.

"Nice ride." Jack shook his head.

"It's only because I promised Colt, not because I'm a big baby."

"Trust me, I know. Anyone that could pull half the stunts you have couldn't possibly be deemed a baby. It explains why Colt's hooked on you."

"He's not hooked. We're just friends."

"If you say so."

The paramedic lifted her out of the car and onto the gurney with ease, tucking the blankets around her and strapping her down. *Totally ridiculous.* But for Colt, she didn't voice her discontent. Dakota watched as he leaned inside his car and pulled out the dog's leash. The dog stopped barking, as if happy everyone seemed to finally get the message. But Dakota couldn't leave yet, not without saying goodbye to her furry best friend and companion.

"Halo, come." The dog barked and ran to her side. Dakota patted his head and gave him a big hug and a kiss when he jumped up, his paws on the gurney. "Be a good boy." Halo seemed to understand, pausing only a moment before he took off toward Colt.

Halo grabbed Colt by his shirt sleeve. *Interesting.* She wondered if Colt even understood the significance of the action. Halo was trained to sense discomfort and was clearly trying to find a new way to communicate with Colt other than grabbing Colt's hand in his mouth. Halo's teeth could be a bit disconcerting, even if the dog was as gentle as a kitten when he did it.

"Good boy." Colt reached out to pat the dog.

Dakota was proud of Halo for understanding Colt and meeting his needs.

"Well, I'll be danged. Apparently, Halo didn't get the message Colt's not a fan of dogs." Jack grinned.

"Or maybe he knows and is trying hard to correct that." Dakota shrugged. "Knowing Halo, I'm banking on my guess."

"I hate to break up everyone's little get together, but we're ready to roll. We need to get her to the hospital." The paramedic started to push her toward the ambulance.

"Fine. Let's get this over with," she muttered.

Dakota watched Halo, Colt, and Jack, right up until the doors closed and blocked her view. She said a prayer for their safe return as the siren was flipped on and they headed for the hospital.

Chapter Fourteen

♥

"THERE." COLT POINTED TO the Cliff Walk vista Dakota had told him about. He pushed Halo back as he tried to crawl into the front seats. "Hang on, boy."

"Someone's revved up to get this search started." Jack laughed.

"Looks that way." Colt slid out of the car and opened the back door. Halo bounded out, tail wagging like this was a training mission.

"Easy, boy. This is the real thing. Your chance to show off what you've learned." Colt hooked the leash to his collar. "Hey, Jack, grab Dakota's sweater, will you?"

"Got it." Jack came around the car and joined them.

"Thanks. All right, Halo. Time to do your thing. Get a good whiff." Colt held the sweater up to Halo's nose. Almost immediately, the dog growled. "Good boy. That's it. Now go find Mateo."

The dog started to sniff the ground and look around. When he started to pull against the hold Colt had on the leash, he turned and barked.

"Turn him loose, Colt."

"Are you crazy? Dakota will kill me if he gets lost."

"You need to trust him to do his job."

"Fine. Let's hope you're right." Colt unhooked the leash, and Halo took off running, his nose to the ground. He systematically seemed to cover the ground while Colt and Jack waited. The wait seemed to take forever, but he knew without a scent to follow, the search would be harder and be far more time consuming.

Halo stopped and let out a bark, turning back to them to tell them he'd found something.

"Good boy." Jack and Colt went running to where the dog waited. The minute they got close, Halo was off and running in the direction of the scent he'd picked up. Every now and then he would stop to wait for them, but then he'd take off again with renewed zest when they closed the distance. They followed what looked to be a rarely used trail, some of the overgrowth making it harder to get through.

They came to a juncture where Halo had stopped and sat while he waited. Colt rubbed the dog's side and gave him a pat. "Here. Get another good whiff." He pressed the sweater to the dog's nose.

Halo moved ahead tentatively, as if not sure. He went back and forth between the two trails, widening his territory each time.

"Looks like he lost the trail. We could split up here and keep in touch with what we discover." Colt couldn't help the disappointment that settled in over him. Visions of Halo leading them right to Mateo dissipated.

"I don't like it. Mateo could be holed up anywhere. We need to stick together. Let's just pick one and pray it's right. We've got a fifty-fifty shot."

"Yeah, but it's the fifty percent wrong I'm worried about." Colt shook his head, not liking the odds.

"I hear you. Which way you want to go?"

Halo was still running through the woods, sniffing some of the underbrush near the trail.

"Left." His stomach clenched. The thought of this guy escaping was upsetting, but the idea of Mateo getting back to Dakota put an even greater fear in him. A fear greater than even when the thug's trained killer dog had him by the throat.

"Halo, come," Colt called after the dog who was currently sniffing something on the other trail. He and Jack started down the path, knowing Halo would follow. Colt glanced back for confirmation, but this time the dog hadn't followed. "Hold up, Jack."

They stopped to watch Halo. His nose was practically glued to the ground as he moved farther up the path. Halo let out a bark and took off running.

"Well, I'll be, the dog's picked up Mateo's scent again." Colt shook his head; relieved things were back on track.

"Remind me not to bet on you for anything, you're not such a good guesser." Jack laughed, and they took off running to catch up to Halo. The dog slowed down, looking back occasionally to see where they were. They were deep in the woods, and he couldn't help wondering where the trail led. Mateo certainly had them at an advantage there.

"We've been making good time, and Mateo couldn't have had more than a fifteen to twenty-minute lead. Plus, he doesn't know he's being chased. We might exercise a little more caution going forward."

"I agree. Let's call Halo back so he doesn't tip Mateo off." Colt let out a low whistle, deciding against calling out for him.

Halo came trotting back and sat at his side. "Good boy." Colt ruffled his fur. He gave the dog a fresh sniff of Dakota's sweater. "Easy, boy. Heel." The men took off, side by side, with Halo walking just in front of them.

Five minutes passed before Colt stopped to wipe the sweat from his brow and to glance around. The place all looked the same. Huge trees, lots of undergrowth, and no sign of life.

Halo growled and crouched low to the ground. Colt wasn't an experienced dog handler, but a good guess told him the dog had picked up on something different. The dog crawled forward through the underbrush. In a clearing off in the distance, Colt spotted a cabin and pointed it out to Jack. No words were necessary.

Halo's low growl was enough to confirm they were in the right place. Colt pulled out his gun, and Jack did the same. "Halo, stay," he commanded the dog, not wanting him to get mixed up in the arrest. Dakota told him Mateo had a gun and they needed to proceed with caution. The man clearly had no qualms about killing someone, having done it at least twice, and with a third attempt.

He shoved back against all thoughts of what might have happened to Dakota had he not gotten to her in time and tried to focus. Halo did as he was told, not moving an inch.

Jack waved his gun, indicating he intended to circle around the back of the building.

Colt nodded and started forward, keeping low and behind the bushes to stay out of sight. They closed in, but there was still no sign of Mateo.

A shot rang out, the sound far too close for Colt's liking. He ducked behind the largest tree and took aim, trying to pinpoint where Mateo was located. He couldn't see Jack, but he knew his partner would have heard the shot. Another shot was fired, this time off to the left.

Colt took aim and fired, hoping to engage Mateo's attention as Jack made his move and circled around behind him. He heard another sound and swung around to discover Halo had crept closer, his eyes trained forward. "Good boy." Colt patted his head. "I know, it's hard not to get in on the action, isn't it? You've got to stay though. I can't let anything happen to you." Halo licked his hand. "Stay, boy."

Moving closer to the cabin, Colt thought he spotted movement and headed in the opposite direction. Mateo was on the run. There was no way he was going to let him get away. Colt fired in the general direction he'd spotted him, hoping to flush him out.

Three more answering shots were fired, all hitting the cabin. Mateo wasn't far away. Jack came around from the other side and motioned to him that he would cut wide and try to get behind. There was a good chance Mateo didn't know Jack was out there since he hadn't fired in his direction at all.

Colt moved forward again, not wanting to let Mateo gain too much ground.

Another shot rang out, this one not in his direction at all. It sounded as if Mateo might have figured out there were two of them.

Halo suddenly went charging passed him toward where Mateo had disappeared. "Halo, no.

Come, boy." The dog was already out of range and didn't slow. This wouldn't end well if he didn't get to the dog first. Colt took off running.

On and on, he ran, until he didn't have a clue where he was running. There was no sign of Mateo, Halo, or Jack. He stopped to assess the situation and took a deep breath. He had to find Halo.

A branch snapped behind him, and Colt swung around. Mateo stood there; his gun trained on Colt. This wasn't going to end well. Where was Jack when he needed him? One clean shot would put an end to Mateo, and the world would be rid of the scum bag.

"You again." Mateo snarled.

"Nice of you to remember me. This is private property and you're trespassing." Colt was trying to stall, hoping Jack would catch up.

"This is public state-owned land. Nice try. Where's your partner? He might want to think twice about coming any closer, or I'll put a bullet in you."

"He may have turned back." Colt lied.

"Why are you chasing me? I'm a free man and this could be considered harassment," Mateo ground out.

There was no way he'd tell the man about Dakota. The other truth seemed like a better option now. "You're a suspect in the Wingate Collection heist that happened in New York."

"*Ahhh*. You two have it all wrong. Someone should have told you, the jewels I have are fakes. No crime in that." Colt wanted to wipe the smug grin right off his face.

"Sounds like I missed the memo. No harm, no foul. Mind if I put a call through to verify your story? Just in case you've escaped, and I need we need to haul you back in." Out of the corner of his eye, he saw Halo. He shook his head, trying to send the dog a message, all the while knowing it wouldn't help.

"Big talk for a man not in control. You must think I'm stupid. There's no way you're walking out of here alive. I just need to make it look good. Perhaps a bullet through the heart, followed by one from your own gun so it will look like suicide."

"Sounds like a specialty of yours," Colt snapped.

"What's that supposed mean?" Mateo took a step forward.

"Nothing. Just sounds like this isn't your first time out."

"Mind your own business. Head for the cabin. Let's hope for your sake your partner's lost."

There wasn't much choice at this point but to do what he was told. Colt turned and headed back toward the cabin.

Halo's familiar growl reached his ears. Colt swung around just as Halo launched himself at Mateo, who had turned the gun on the dog. The boom of the gunshot echoed all around.

"No!" Colt ran toward the Halo. The dog hadn't let go of Mateo, and Colt didn't see any blood. The shot must have missed, whereas the dog's aim was perfect.

Mateo screamed in pain and dropped the gun just as Jack came running through the woods.

"Freeze, Mateo." Jack ran up, his gun never wavering off the thug.

"It's about time you showed up. Looks like I found me a new partner." Colt shot Jack a look of relief.

"He's got four legs so he's twice as fast, but he can't shoot." Jack grinned as he unclipped a set of handcuffs and tossed them at Colt.

"By the looks of it, he doesn't need a gun. Those teeth are doing the trick." Colt shook his head, remembering all too well the feel of another dog's teeth, but this time, it didn't bring on the sickening fear he'd come to associate with the memory.

"Halo, leave it. Come, boy." Halo stilled and then let go of Mateo's arm. He came to sit next to Colt. "Good boy."

Colt cuffed the scumbag and pulled him to his feet, Mateo letting loose a string of expletives that would curl the hairs of his dead grandmother. "I'll call it in and have them rendezvous at the cabin. There must be a road closer than the way we came in."

"Roger." Jack pushed Mateo toward the cabin. "Get a move on. There's a prison cell waiting for the likes of you."

Halo lay down next to him, resting his head on his two front paws. Colt called for backup, explained the situation, and then hung up. Halo's light whimper captured his attention. He knelt beside the dog and ran a hand down his side, making sure the bullet hadn't nicked Halo.

"What is it, boy? Are you hurt?" Halo whimpered. Satisfied there was no open wound, Colt ran a hand down each of the dog's legs. When he got to the back right paw, Halo pulled away, his whimper intensifying.

He needed to get Halo to the vet and have him look at the paw. He hoped it was nothing more serious than a sprain, probably from the long jump when he took Mateo down. Colt needed to call Dakota, but the thought of how the call would go brought up mixed emotions. She would be relieved Mateo would soon be back behind bars. But when he told her to meet them at the vet instead of back at the house... Well, that part he was sure would torment her until she could meet up with them and see for herself that Halo would be okay.

Chapter Fifteen

♥

DAKOTA HAD TROUBLE CONVINCING the security officer she was free to leave and that his services were no longer needed, but there was no way she was sticking around to wait for Colt to call him. The guy could follow her for all she cared, but nothing would stop her from meeting Colt at the Redwood Cove Veterinary Clinic where he was taking Halo.

Colt said it looked like a sprained paw and not to worry. *Not worry. Hah! Not possible.*

Being an FBI agent didn't make him a vet. Until Dr. Keller gave her the verdict of what was wrong, she'd withhold the right to stay worried.

She drove across town, careful to not accidentally use her right foot, which made things difficult when it came to driving. But Halo needed her, and nothing could keep her from going to him. Her faithful companion was always there for her, and now, it was her turn. Maybe she shouldn't have let him go in the first place.

Dakota parked, briefly noting the security officer's car pulling in beside her. She hobbled to the front door, still trying to get used to the crutch she would need to use for a bit. "Where are they, Maria?" The receptionist looked up, smiled, held up a finger, and then placed a call on hold.

"In room two. Who's the hunky guy who brought Halo in?"

"*Umm*, a friend of mine." Dakota wasn't sure how much she should reveal. The door opened behind her with a jingle of the bells. Her security officer stood there glaring at her.

"Before you say anything, talk to Colt. He's here. He'll verify exactly what I told you."

"Fine. I'll wait here until he comes out." The burly man stood, feet apart, blocking the door.

"Suit yourself." Dakota turned, ignoring the questioning look on Maria's face. She headed for room two, eager to get to Halo. Without knocking, she pushed open the door with her shoulder. Halo was on the table, his back paw wrapped in a bandage, Colt hovering close by to help hold him.

"Oh, my poor baby. Are you okay?" She moved to the table to pet him, shooting the doctor a tell-me-everything look.

"Looks like Halo suffered a sprain to his back paw. He'll be fine."

"Thank goodness." Dakota let out a deep breath of relief and nuzzled her cheek against Halo's head. The dog turned and licked her face, his wet, doggy kiss a welcome gesture of affection.

"I told you not to worry," Colt's deep voice cut into their cheerful reunion.

She gazed up at him and smiled. "The day you have a veterinarian degree hanging on your office wall is the day I'll believe you when you diagnose an animal's injury."

"Fair enough." He grinned. "Doc was just finishing up. What do you say we get him back to your place so he can rest?"

"Can we make it your place? It's quieter there, and I really want to talk with you about what happened. Oh, and your security goon is out their standing guard at the front door. You might want to let him go home."

"Will do. Let me send him on his way and I'll be back to carry Halo to the truck."

"Okay. I can talk to Dr. Keller and get the home-care instructions."

Colt left, and Dakota turned her full attention to the doctor. A week for healing wasn't too bad, and then life could return to normal.

Well, almost normal. Colt would be gone. Somehow, in the short time she'd known him, she'd come to care for the guy. More than she would have thought possible. She'd miss him, but she also knew he had a job in L.A. waiting for him. It figured that when she finally found someone she could trust and might consider dating; he'd live seven hours away and be married to his job.

"We're done here. Stop at the front desk and make an appointment for me to check him over next week."

"Thanks, Doc."

True to his word, Colt returned minutes later. "All set?" He picked Halo up, and Dakota held open the door. "Are you sure you're okay? I can come back and carry you to the car if you need me to."

"I'll be fine. I'm quickly moving to expert level on this wooden leg. Which vehicle is yours?"

"One of the officers let me borrow his truck. It's the black Chevy over there." Colt nodded his head in the general direction.

"It might be more comfortable for him to ride with you. I'll follow you to your place in my aunt's car. She's letting me borrow it for as long as I need it." She held open the door of the truck.

"You drove here...with your foot the way it is? That was dangerous. You could have just had your security detail drive you in. You need to ride with me. I'll get someone to fetch the car later." Colt leaned in and dropped a kiss on her cheek, surprising her.

He was right and she hated it. But more than that, his kiss had her ready to agree. "Okay." It was Colt's turn to look surprised. Ten minutes later, they pulled into the driveway behind him. Dakota fumbled with her crutches to get out of the car and then hobbled her way toward him to take the keys. "I'll get the door."

Colt leaned in to pick Halo up, carried him into the house, and set him down gently on the couch. What had happened to the Colt who didn't care for dogs? Halo had him wrapped up in knots of concern and caring.

Once they had the dog settled, Dakota took a deep breath and exhaled slowly, practicing one of her mediation moves.

It was over. *All of it.*

Mateo was back in jail, she had her mother's jewelry, and Halo was safe. She crossed her arms together in front of her chest, forcing herself to accept it was real.

Colt moved to stand in front of her and held open his arms. It was an invitation to security and warmth, and an invitation she wasn't about to refuse.

She stepped into his arms, loving the strength of his embrace. Slowly, the tension began to ebb from her body, but with it, the tears followed. Tired of holding it together for so long, Dakota couldn't fight the surge of emotions filling her. Years of repressed heartache broke down the wall she'd built around her heart as she thought of her parents, and the loss their deaths had brought to the family. *She missed them so much.*

She cried until there was nothing left to cry. And through it all, Colt simply held her, not saying a word. When she lifted her head, she noticed her tears had left a huge wet area on his shirt. Dakota reached up to touch the spot, knowing it was the mark of her healing. "Sorry," she choked out.

"Don't worry about it. It'll dry. You doing okay?" he asked.

"I'm better. Thanks to you."

"I'm just doing my job." His comment stung a little.

"I know. But men don't usually handle emotional women very well."

"Men might not, but I want to be here for you, Dakota."

She moved to sit on the couch, finding it easy to talk to Colt.

He came and sat next to her, enveloping her hand in his.

Years of keeping everything bottled up inside came pouring out as she told him about her parents. About the fun times and about the years after they died. Selective amnesia may have kept her from remembering what Victor looked like, but it hadn't stopped any of the pain of all the other memories, and it didn't stop the guilt she felt for not being able to help the police find the guy who'd broken into their home.

It felt good to be curled up in his arms. Safe.

Stretching up, Dakota pressed her lips to his mouth. Tentative at first, she increased the pressure, encouraged when he didn't pull away.

Colt reached up to touch her face, cupping her face softly. He moved to kiss her forehead before settling back on the sofa. His message was clear. He was here for her emotionally but wouldn't take advantage of her physically. It made her like and respect him even more, if that were possible.

"Can I ask you something?"

"Ask away."

"You and Halo, you're different now. Does that mean you're over what happened before?"

Colt tensed, took a deep breath, and then relaxed, his hand going to where Halo lay next to him. "I think so. But the scars, they'll never go away. It's why I wear high-neck polo shirts."

Dakota blanched. Scars on the neck meant a dog would have had him by the throat. There was no need to hear any more, the vivid image plenty. "I'm so sorry."

He took her hand in his and pulled down the neck of his shirt, placing her hand against the scars. She sensed her reaction was important and stayed strong.

Letting her fingers caress the raised welts, she massaged the area with every ounce of tenderness she possessed.

Colt watched her closely. "Thanks for not...um, reacting. They aren't pretty, and you're the first person I've shared this much with."

His trust in her blew her away. He had to care about her to share something so personal, didn't he? "It's a part of who you are, and I like you."

"I like you, too. To answer your question about Halo, I think he's been working his therapy magic on me ever since I met him. But when he put his life on the line for me, the connection fell into place."

"That's how I felt when he came to me. The bond we shared was special, and I trusted it."

"I get it. I fell in love with him in that moment." Colt smiled.

And Dakota had fallen in love with Colt. He was the kind of man she'd been looking for all her life, one who reminded her of the love her mother and father shared, one who might very well be the hero of her life.

The part Colt didn't tell Dakota was that he'd also connected with her. Telling her would complicate everything.

Dakota had nestled up against him and fallen asleep. She looked relaxed, more relaxed than he remembered seeing her since he'd known her. He hated to disturb her, but there was no way they could stay like this long. His arm would go numb within the hour.

Colt edged away and picked her up, carrying her down the hall to his bedroom. He laid her down and started to pull away, but she clung to him.

"Stay," she murmured.

He lay down on the bed with her, pulling her into his arms, being careful to avoid contact with her right foot. She snuggled closer.

Colt valued the trust she'd placed in him, telling things she'd long since buried deep inside. Together, with Halo by her side, Dakota had finally laid the past to rest. She was a strong woman and would finally have the chance to move on with her life. It gave him a sense of satisfaction to know he'd been able to help. Remembering back to when he'd first noticed her during the surveillance, it was then he'd recognized a sadness about her and had wanted to do nothing more than erase the look from her face.

Colt knew he'd have to leave and go back to L.A. soon, but he didn't want to let her go, not just yet. Not while he was still undecided about everything. There was no place for a woman in his life with the career he'd chosen. Others did it quite successfully, but it wasn't a risk he was willing to take. Dakota had been through enough, and asking her to face the dangers that came with his job was out of the question.

Besides, she had a life here. A good one. She was surrounded by family and friends and was part owner of a successful family business. There was no way he could even ask her to give it all up.

The only option would be for him to move here. The fact he was even considering it as an option meant he was in more trouble than he could have imagined. Was it possible he'd fallen in love? He'd be forced to leave the FBI, something he wasn't sure he was prepared to do. It was all he knew, and he'd earned every promotion he'd gotten by hard work and long hours.

The sexy thief had gotten under his skin and stolen his heart. Too bad he couldn't let her keep it. Regrettably, there was no way it could work.

Colt had no idea how much sleep he'd gotten, but as the early morning light filtered through the window, he knew it was past time to check in with the office. He slid out of the bed, trying not to disturb her. Pausing at the door, he watched her for a few minutes, loving the way her raven hair cascaded over his pillow.

Halo looked up at him from where he slept curled up against her. His tail thumped the bed. Dakota was his life, and together with Halo, they were his family. A family he had to protect, and that meant leaving.

Colt left the room to check his phone. Jack's messages confirmed Mateo was in jail in Redwood Cove, awaiting charges to be filed—which meant Colt needed to get a move on. The paperwork alone would bury him at the office for days as he sought to unravel all the details and properly document everything.

There was no way Victor Mateo was going to beat this rap and be back on the streets. If the recording Dakota taped was even remotely close to a full disclosure of the murders he'd committed, then Mateo was going away for a long time. And if they could find the Wingate jewels, there would be several other charges to tag on to the sentence.

He would have to come clean about the letting Dakota reclaim her family's stolen jewels, but it would be worth it if she got justice for all the wrongs Victor had committed against her family. A reprimand would more than likely mar his record, but in the name of justice, he'd let it happen. And if he had the choice to do it over, he'd give her the five minutes all over again. Doing crazy things was sometimes all that drove you to the finish line in this business.

Returning to the room, he crossed to the bed and sat down. Brushing her cheek with his hand, he tried to wake her. "Dakota, I have to leave."

She stirred and moved closer to him. He leaned down to kiss her cheek. "I hate to go like this, honey, but I've got to head back to LA. Can you hear me?"

"I hear you," she mumbled. "I wish you'd stay."

"With Victor in custody, the boss is blowing up my phone wanting me to file my reports and get back to the office. The state police are transporting him to a tighter security prison until he goes to trial."

"What charges?" Her eyes flew open, piercing him with her gaze.

He knew why Dakota was asking. She needed to hear the words for reassurance. "Two counts murder, one count attempted murder, one count of kidnapping, and one count grand larceny for your mother's jewelry, which by the way, was a charge we initially couldn't have brought against him since you had possession of the jewelry. Your testimony and the recording will be enough to charge him. Provided of course you can tell me where to find your phone and that the recording of his admission of guilt will hold up in court."

"Oh, it will hold up all right. It's on my desk...right where I left it. Are you still going after him for the Wingate heist?"

"We've got enough to put him away without it, and since the jewels were fake, we don't have a case." It was the one part of the whole deal he didn't like, because he was convinced Mateo had had something to do with the disappearance of the Wingate collection.

"Wait a minute. Victor said something about other more valuable jewels that I didn't take. It was how he knew it was me. There was another box in the safe, but I only wanted what was mine. Could the real Wingate jewels still be there?" she asked, her eyes glazed with hope.

What were the odds? If she was right, it would save the case and his reputation, and it would offset his slight error of judgement in letting Dakota pursue her own interests that night. "It's possible."

"Let's go get them together. If they're there, you can take them with you." She flung the covers back and eased out of bed, testing her ankle.

"Not so fast. This time, we get a search warrant." Her excitement was contagious, but he'd be going by the book.

"No fun." She pouted.

"Yeah, but way more legal." He dropped a kiss on her lips. "If you're going with me, you better get a move on."

"You mean it? I can go?" Lord, how he loved her sweet smile.

"If you hurry, yes. But this time, you can only watch. Do you remember the combination? It would make it a whole lot easier for all of us." Colt could always say he took her with him this time based on her expertise. Who else could tell him in minutes if they were genuine or not?

"Of course, I remember it. I remember every-thing. Eventually." He knew exactly what she meant. For her, this all started when she saw Victor's picture in the tabloid and remembered the tattoo. Luckily, she was on his side, because Dakota was one heck of a force to be reckoned with when she decided she wanted something.

"As a key witness, you do realize you'll need protection until this case comes to court?"

"Only if it's you." He felt the same way, but he knew it wouldn't be that easy.

"That's not the way it works with the FBI. They have guys who specialize in witness protection. Besides, I'll be in L.A." He saw the hurt in her eyes, and it about killed him not to take her in his arms. It was better this way, even if it didn't feel right.

Chapter Sixteen

♥

Halo didn't like being left behind this time around, but with his injury, Dakota wasn't about to let him tag along. The doctor had ordered rest, and rest he would get. Watching him limp around this morning was a stark reminder of everything that had happened, but at least now, the reminders didn't come with a stark wrenching heartache. All thanks to Colt, Jack, and Halo.

"How's the foot this morning?" Colt asked.

"Better. The ice packs have done wonders. I'm going to try and ditch the crutch today and see how it goes."

"Are you sure that's a good idea?"

"It'll be fine. Quit worrying." Dakota wanted to reassure him, knowing it wouldn't take much for him to override her decision.

"Okay, then. I trust your judgement. Can you follow me in your car, or would that be too much? I promised the agent I'd return his truck today, and since I already know you can drive with one foot if needed." He grinned. "The bureau should be delivering a new car for me sometime this morning, so it would be great if I could catch a ride back here with you."

"No problem. I don't mind playing chauffer after all that you've done for me. Including last night. Thanks, Colt. It meant a lot to me." She reached out to touch his arm, letting him know how she felt with actions and words. The guy had been a loner for such a long time, he needed to know people cared about him and to hear the good he did for others. To understand the good he brought to other's lives. Unfortunately, it was also the reason she would have to let him go. There were plenty of others who needed his help.

"Don't say another word. It meant a lot to me, too." His hand closed over hers, his warmth filling her with mixed emotions. Colt reminded her of her father. A good man. One a woman could trust and share her life with.

But not once had he mentioned returning from L.A to see her. Or the date they'd scheduled before he would leave. Not a word. He was determined to wrap up business in Redwood Cove and head home, their plans forgotten.

Dakota followed him to the Mateo residence and parked behind his truck on the street. She shuddered, remembering the last time she was here and what it had led up to. *No more.* Shoving the memory aside, she grabbed her backpack and fell in step with Colt as they walked up the driveway.

"Remember not to touch anything. This is still a cordoned off area being investigated."

"I promise. I'll stay right behind you and be a good girl." She grinned. Teasing him was fast becoming something she rather enjoyed.

He opened the door and stepped inside. Several uniformed officers stepped forward to greet them.

Colt flashed his badge. "Colt Jackson. Lead investigator on the case."

The two men nodded and stepped aside. "Great job nailing Mateo." The policeman on the right spoke first.

"Yeah, the guy always managed to fly under the radar around here and used his money to buy himself out of prosecution a few times. From what I hear, you got him good."

"You can say that again. Mateo isn't getting a get-out-of-jail-free card this time." Colt started up the stairs.

The man on the left stepped in front of Dakota.

"I'm with him." She pointed at Colt.

Colt stopped and turned back. "She's with me, and I've given her a rundown of the rules."

"Good enough." The two men let her pass, and she headed up the stairs.

"Nervous?" Colt asked.

"No. Not a bit. The place is crawling with police officers, but more importantly, I've got you."

Colt shot her a glance, his brow furrowed, but then continued up the stairs without a word.

What was that about? She didn't have time to think it through, but later, she had every intention of trying to figure him out. They entered Victor's study, where several other officers were dusting for prints and taking photos for the investigation.

"Hey, guys, this is Dakota. She's convinced the Wingate collection is still here, and I've brought her along to identify if they're the real deal. Let's hope she's right."

Everyone either nodded or murmured hello, and Dakota smiled. "Where's Jack?"

"He should be here anytime. There's no way he wanted to miss this before going home to the wife. She'd never let him live it down if he didn't come home with pictures."

"He's married?" Dakota was shocked. It would seem not everyone shared Colt's views on work and family.

"Yes." One short word. Zero elaboration. Typical Colt style when he didn't want to talk about something.

"Then let's get down to business." She tossed her bag on the desk and pulled out her gloves, careful to follow his rules.

Colt had also pulled on a pair of gloves and removed the photo from wall. "What's the combo?"

"Twenty-two. Ninety. Eight-nine. Start clockwise," she recited the numbers forever etched in her brain.

Colt turned the dial back and forth to the numbers and pulled the door open when he finished. He pointed his flashlight into the safe, the light landing on the box she'd noticed last time.

Dakota nodded, letting him know it was the right one. She held her breath, hoping her hunch was right, as much for Colt as herself, and of course, for the duchess.

The box closely matched the size of the safe. Colt reached in, pulled it out, and set it on the desk. Everyone had gathered around to watch.

Colt looked up at her, smiled, and gestured toward the box. "Have at it." He was letting her have the honors, and the gesture touched her heart. If she wasn't already half in love with him, this would have sealed it.

She nodded again, adrenaline racing through her body as she grabbed her loupe from the backpack and laid it beside the box.

Dakota removed the lid and peeled back the black velvet, revealing the most gorgeous hand-crafted pieces of jewelry she'd ever seen. The Wingate collection was stunning. It was exactly like the fake set Victor had created, but there was one major difference—this collection was alive. The blood-red rubies shimmered in the light of the room, the stones telling their own story.

There was little need to inspect them to know they were the real deal, but she picked up her loupe. As a professional, she would do her job, loving every second awarded her to become one with such masterpieces.

No one spoke. They all waited and watched. Colt stood by her side and gave her shoulder a squeeze, letting her know he understood her need to go slowly and savor every second.

She picked up piece after piece, each one proving her right. They were the real deal. The centerpiece of the necklace was an eight-carat ruby—one of the largest in the world and worth millions. Dakota let out a deep breath and nodded when she was finished.

"They are all authentic, and I can certify without a doubt this is the Wingate collection."

Colt hugged her in his excitement, a sentiment she echoed. The rest of the guys looked on in amazement, a few snapping pictures as a keepsake, Jack one of them.

"As much as I hate to end this moment, we need to wrap it up here. I'm calling for extra security to transport the collection back to headquarters where we need to take it in and log it as evidence."

"Thanks for letting me share in this. I know what it means to you, and what it will mean to the duchess. I can't imagine the heartache of having these stolen." Dakota carefully folded the velvet back over the top, hating to cover such beauty.

She turned to hand the box to Colt, who was on the phone.

"Yes, sir. Right away." He slid the phone into his back pocket.

Dakota handed him the box, and their fingers touched. Awareness sizzled between them.

"Good job. The boss sends his thanks for your assistance in cracking this case as well." Colt was a consummate professional in his response with everyone listening.

"Guess that means you're not in trouble any-more?" Torn between the professional and the man, she couldn't help but tease him, preferring to connect with the man.

"Guess not." He laughed. The others had gone back to what they were doing, their efforts renewed after the discovery of evidence that would take Mateo down on more charges.

"We need to get going. I've got a two-patrol car escort back to my place where some other bureau guys are going to meet up with me for the escort to L.A."

"You're leaving immediately?"

"Yes. You knew it had to happen. The security of these jewels has become my number one priority."

"I know. We just never got that date. And you haven't said a thing about coming back." Regret flashed in his eyes, but one of the guys came up to ask him a question, preventing him from answering. And then his phone rang.

She waited, hoping he'd say something. Anything about them.

When he hung up the phone and looked at her, the resigned look on his face was clear. There would be no date.

"Dakota, about earlier...you know—"

"Don't worry. I've known all along you had to return to L.A. I've got Halo, and we'll be just fine." She had to let him go, and it was better if he never knew how she felt. Better for them both.

"He's a great dog, and I've no doubt he'll take great care of you. This is for the best. I'm sorry, but I really need to get going. The duchess wants to personally thank me, and I've been instructed to fly to New York City immediately after I get to L.A and file the proper reports. The boss thinks it's good for our image considering the embarrassment the heist caused in the first place. Our security team is working with the insurance people for the safe transport of the collection. If you follow us back to the house, you can get Halo."

"Sure." She fought back the wave of tears threatening to fall.

Dakota followed the police cruisers back to his place. It was like a motorcade procession for a funeral. And in a way it felt like one, knowing Colt was leaving and whatever existed between them would die a natural death.

Halo was excited to see them, limping his way over as they came through the door. But that's where the excitement ended. Colt was tense and reserved, much like the way she was feeling.

"Come on, boy, it's time to go home." Halo stopped and looked back and forth between her and Colt, not understanding what was happening. He barked and then lay on the floor by the door, refusing her command.

Colt pat Halo's head and stroked his fur. "You be a good boy and go with Dakota. Take care of her for me." Words of goodbye. Forever.

Halo whimpered in understanding and then got up and followed her out the door. She forced herself not to look back. If she did, she might try to make him change his mind. But nothing had changed. He had his life in L.A., and she had her life here. He was right. It was better this way.

If only her heart would agree.

Chapter Seventeen

♥

COLT TOSSED HIS BAG in the back seat of the car and headed for home. Back to the hustle and bustle of the city and its twenty-four-seven action. Taking the scenic route down Highway 17, he slowed down as he passed Cliff Walk. Memories assailed him, both good and bad. He shook his head and smiled. Dakota was both crazy and beautiful, but it was a powerful combination that appealed to him.

The look in her eyes was dangerous when she'd asked about the date. Colt knew she cared, but it wasn't right to foster those feelings, and he should have never pressed her for a date in the first place. No good could have come from it.

Off to his right, Colt spotted a couple of whales headed north. A pair. No. Make that a family. He spotted the calf sticking close to his mother's side. They were magnificent and free to roam the seas. Together. God had created pairs of everything for life to continue. But what did that say about him? A guy who chose to walk through life alone.

The overtures of the song playing on the radio filtered through to his brain. "I Left My Heart in San Francisco"—the words played over and over in his head. Whoever wrote the song, *almost* got it right. The truth was, he'd left his heart in Redwood Cove.

Six hours later, he pulled into the headquarters parking lot, no closer to feeling better about leaving than he had when he'd first left. After passing through security, he headed straight for the captain's office.

"Great job, Colt. A little unorthodox, but the results are good." The captain shook his hand.

"Yes, sir." Colt grinned.

"I've booked you on Delta's ten-fifteen red-eye flight tonight. You'll land in La Guardia at seven-thirty in the morning Eastern Standard time. I've arranged a limo for you on the other end, and the duchess is expecting you by eight-thirty. I appreciate you agreeing to do this. The media will be all over this and we need the good publicity."

"Not a problem. I just need a quick change of clothes and to repack, and I'm ready."

"That's what I love about you, Colt. Always ready to tackle the next job. No wife and kids to tie you down or to coordinate everything with. Not like the rest of us. Speaking of which, the wife is waiting for me. She's called four times for updates on when I'm leaving the office and she can serve dinner." He shook his head and chuckled.

Sounded nice to Colt. Someone at home who cared when you were coming and going and someone to share a meal with at night. And someone to hold every night and wake up with each morning. Someone...like Dakota.

The captain's phone rang. "Make that five." He grinned. "Your tickets are on your desk. I'm gone." He waved and headed for the elevator, but Colt could still hear the captain answer the phone.

"Hey, honey. I'm on my way now. Love you, too."

The words hit hard. The captain was balancing both aspects of his live and obviously doing a great job of it. Colt looked around the office. Six o'clock, and it looked like a ghost town. A few stragglers were still glued to their desks. Men like him. Single men. The rest of the guys and ladies had gone home to be with their families. Somewhere along the line, a lot of them had gotten married and started a new stage of their life. Settling down.

But not Colt. The Lone Ranger. Even Jack had a wife to get home to.

The trip to New York would be good for him, and it was coming at a good time. For the second time in days, he was considering giving it all up. His job. His home. And his life in L.A.

Redwood Cove and a certain raven-haired beauty were calling his name and his heart.

Colt's trip home from New York was uneventful. He'd finished the paperwork updates on the case while on the plane and was looking forward to a few days off. The minute he walked in the door, he felt it. The loneliness.

Before, the quiet had greeted him like an old friend. Now, it echoed around him like a death knell, reinforcing the decision he'd made on the flight home. It was time to retire from the bureau and start a new chapter in his life. One that made room for others, or more specifically, Dakota.

For Colt, retiring was the only way to balance his life because he still wasn't willing to put Dakota in the line of danger that came with his job. As a private investigator, the job was still dangerous at times, but less likely to follow him home at night. The biggest plus to the change, however, was setting his own schedule and being there for the woman he loved, and maybe, one day, his family.

His mother had been happy before his dad died. Her unhappiness was due to missing him after he was killed in the line of duty. It was the same unhappiness he finally realized he was feeling, but it wasn't something he needed to accept. Dakota was still very much alive, and he was sure she cared about him, too.

The next few days were busy. Colt turned in his resignation, much to the consternation of his captain, and arranged for office space in Redwood Cove. Whether Dakota accepted what he had to offer or not, it was time for him to slow down and enjoy more of life. Besides, even if she said no, by living in Redwood Cove, he'd have plenty of opportunities to change her mind. There was no way he'd give up easily.

The car was packed, and Colt headed north to Redwood Cove and his new home. He'd found the perfect place overlooking the ocean, a place that could accommodate a new family when and if needed. Sooner than later, hopefully.

Hours later, he pulled into the Cliff Walk vista where he'd first officially met Dakota. He pulled out his phone and dialed her number.

"Hello, stranger. I was hoping I'd hear from you some time."

Her breathless voice enchanted him, and it home how much he'd missed her.

"I take it as a good sign that you recognized my number." He chuckled.

"It's the ring tone I assigned to you." He could almost see the smile on her face.

"Dare I ask?"

"*License to Kill*, of course." The sound of her laughter made his heart skip a beat.

"Of course. Guess you'll be changing the ring tune soon enough." Colt couldn't help but drop a hint, something to encourage her to agree to meet him.

"What's that supposed to mean?"

"How about I tell you over dinner?" He delivered the question as if it were an everyday thing and not a big deal. Except it was a big deal.

"Dinner? When will you be in town? You can't make statements like that and make me wait for days or weeks. We've been through this before...although I would like to thank you in person for having my car fixed. It was such a sweet gesture and completely unexpected."

"It was the least I could do considering I'm the one who wrecked it." There were other reasons, but he'd only know understood to the driving need to make things right for Dakota. She treasured the car and that in itself, was enough reason for him to fix it. "As to dinner...how about tonight? At the Sea Vista. I hear they have the best salmon. I'll pick you up at six and will be looking forward to your personalized version of a thank you." Colt chuckled.

"Tonight? As in, you're in town?" Her voice hitched higher.

"That *would* be how I can pick you up in an hour. If I recall, you owe me a date." He couldn't help but tease her. And he couldn't help the relief flooding him that she was receptive to him at all. He'd packed up and left L.A. and hadn't said a word to her the past two weeks. For the first week, he hadn't known what to say. The second week, he'd been afraid she wouldn't take his call given which is why he'd put everything in place before he dialed her number.

Everything had to be perfect for their first date.

"I said I would cook for you. Two different things."

"Next time."

"Who says there'll be a next time?"

"I'm counting on it."

"Let's start with one and see where it takes us. I haven't heard from you in two weeks. Halo misses you. He'll be happy to see you again."

"Perfect. See you in an hour." Colt hung up, not entirely satisfied with her non-committal answer to a second date. He knew it wouldn't be easy, but it wouldn't stop him from hoping.

He pulled into her driveway right at six, slid out of the classic Ford truck he'd recently purchased, and headed for the door. Before he even had to knock, the door was opened, and Dakota stepped out.

Her raven hair hung loosely around her face, reminding him of when he watched her sleeping. Beautiful. Blue jeans that fit every curve and a white gauze top spoke of a carefree woman who owned the world. Gone were the dress pants and suits. Colt liked the new look. It matched the fresh happiness he felt surrounding her.

Colt leaned in and gave her a hug, breathing in deeply to reacquaint his senses with the scent of her hair. She didn't wear perfume, but her skin and hair carried her own signature scent of vanilla and warmth.

"Hi, there. You look stunning." He grinned.

"You don't look so bad yourself. What's with the jeans?" Dakota flushed prettily.

"Life is about being comfortable. I could ask you the same thing. I don't recall seeing you in jeans either."

"Life *is* comfortable. Thanks to you." She nodded toward the truck. "Where did you get the old Ford? The last I saw, the bureau sent you another Crown Victoria."

"This is mine. I'll explain at the restaurant. Reservations are for six-fifteen, so we need to head out. Where's Halo?" Just as he asked the question, a big golden ball of fur came running out the front door, stopping next to him and dancing excitedly. Colt laughed.

"Hey, boy." He rubbed him behind the ears and knelt beside the dog. "You're looking better. No more bandage is a good sign." He hugged Halo to his side.

He'd missed Dakota and Halo, but after tonight, he was hoping all that would change.

"Glad to see you two are still getting along. I'll put him inside so we can go."

"I'll be back, boy. Maybe you can come to my house soon to play. That is, if your mom agrees."

Colt smiled at Dakota, noticing her sudden look of interest.

"You're full of surprises. Halo, inside." She started to close the door. "Good, boy. I'll be back soon." She petted the dog on the head and shut the door.

Colt took her arm and led her to the truck, opened the passenger door and helped her up inside.

"Wow, this is nice. I didn't know you were into classics."

"There's a lot you don't know, and I aim to correct that. Starting tonight." Classic Fords had been his thing growing up, but it wasn't until now he had the luxury of time to do anything about it. Dakota's Mustang had reminded him of the days he used to play with model cars, and how he'd dreamed of fixing up his own truck.

"Good. There's a lot I want to know."

After they were seated in the restaurant, Colt tried to figure out the best way to broach the subject of his retirement and new business venture, and most importantly, of spending time with her and giving their relationship a real chance to work. In the end, he decided to go for direct—his normal approach.

They placed their orders, and the server poured their wine and then left them alone. Colt reached for her hand.

"I know you've got a lot of questions, but if you'll let me explain, then you can ask me anything else you want to know." Her hand radiated with warmth, and the light in her blue eyes sparkled with what he hoped was love.

"I'm listening. And for the record, I'm glad you're here. I've missed you." Her soft voice and sweet smile made him wonder how he could have ever thought of giving her up.

"I've missed you, too."

"But you never called. That hurt."

Ouch. "I'm sorry. I had to do some soul searching and then some soul redefining first."

"Are you done working on your soul?" Her dimple deepened as she bit back her laugh.

"It's a work in progress." He winked. "You know, I left because of my job, but not calling you is on me. I've never met anyone like you, and I thought about you and what made you different all the way to L.A. It also forced me to realize I've lived my life in a shell, protected by the shield of the bureau." There were a lot of things he thought about on the drive home and in the days that followed, but most of them had centered on missing Dakota.

"I don't understand." The lines across her forehead deepened.

"Let me finish, and I promise it should all make sense. Or I hope it does." He took a deep breath before continuing. "My dad was a police officer. He was shot and killed in the line of duty when I was eight years old. My mother went from a beautiful, full-of-life woman to a sad and lonely widow who never recovered. From my perspective, I was convinced that relationships and family don't mix with law enforcement. And from the very beginning, I wanted to be a cop like my father. I idolized the man. The result is who you see today. Or I should say, who you saw a few weeks ago."

The candlelight flickered, the glow softening her features. Her gaze never faltered as she waited silently for the rest of the story.

"On the way home, I had an epiphany. I realized what they shared before he died was love. A wonderful, magical kind of love. My mother experienced it firsthand, and the joy in her life was shared with others. It was only after he was gone that she became a lonely and unhappy woman. Her life now is the same as mine. She's unhappy because she refuses to live life again. It's a choice. Just like I have a choice. Life has no guarantees, but what I do know is I'd like you in it...to see where things could go between us." He'd never told anyone about his family. Not even Jack knew the real reasons he'd refused the very idea of love and family. But he trusted Dakota with his deepest secret and his deepest fears.

"Wow. That's a lot to take in, but it explains some things I never understood. Thank you for sharing." She squeezed his hand. "And since you've told me what makes you tick, perhaps you should understand me a little better as well. You see, when you left, it hurt. A lot."

"I'm sorry, Dakota. Believe me, please." This conversation wasn't headed in the direction he'd hoped for.

"I do. But because you're the first man I've been around that I felt I could trust; someone I could open my heart to. It's like a first-love kind of heartbreak. After my parents died, I really struggled. Halo has been the magic in my life, and he got me through you leaving, not that I haven't wished things could be different, but I had to get over you and not let my emotions drag me down."

Her words were like a double-edged sword—love and goodbye in the same space of conversation. "Things will be different. I promise."

"But how can I trust in that? You already left once and never called." Dakota pulled her hand from his and sat back in her seat.

He had to find the right words to make her understand. To get her to give them a chance.

"If I don't call you, you have only to stop at the house and read me my rights." Colt smiled, hoping to keep her talking. Hoping to convince her to trust in him again.

"In L.A.?"

"No. Here in Redwood Cove. I bought a place with an ocean view, knowing how much you love the sea and like to watch the whales."

"But how will you commute for your job?" She shook her head, confused in an adorable sort of way. It was time to show his hand and hope it came up aces.

"By normal route. Highway 17 leads right through Main Street and past Jackson Securities, my new private investigator's office." He sat back and waited for the information to sink in.

Dakota ran her hands through her hair, pulling the long tresses together and dropping them down her back. "You quit the FBI? You're telling me you bought a house and live here? And work here?"

"Yes, to all of the above."

"Is there anything else I should know?" She leaned forward, one arm resting on the table. There was a new light in her eyes.

He reached for her hand, letting his thumb rub her palm. Colt could feel the tension radiating from her. Halo wasn't here to calm her worries, but Colt wanted to be the man she turned to for help when she was upset. To be the man she trusted. "I love you."

"Wow.' She tried to pull away, but Colt held fast.

"It is a wow, but don't shut me out. Talk to me. Tell me what you're thinking and feeling."

She seemed hesitant at first. And then it happened. Dakota smiled, one of her genuine, you-drive-me-crazy-but-I-care-about-you-too smiles. "Maybe we should have that second date before you mention love."

"The one where you're going to cook for me?" Colt asked.

"Yes, that one." Her breathless whisper was all he needed to hear for reassurance. She was going to give him a chance.

"Perfect. You can cook at my place and enjoy a fabulous sunset. Dance. Watch a movie. That ought to cover about four dates. Then I'll tell you I love you." He grinned.

"Sounds like a plan. And maybe, if the evening is perfect, I'll tell you I love you, too." Dakota's laughter was the music he'd longed to hear for the past two weeks. It was like coming home.

She loved him.

"I'll hold you to that."

Epilogue

♥

SIX MONTHS LATER...

Mr. and Mrs. Jackson. Plus one. Dakota still couldn't believe she'd gotten pregnant so quickly after they'd gotten married. The past had been laid to rest, and in its place was a new beginning. A new life with Colt and a new baby on the way to celebrate that life together. Little John or Chloe would be loved and cherished the same way her parents had loved and cherished her.

Dakota was nervous about the upcoming trial and facing Victor again, but Colt would be right there with her. He assured her that every one of the charges would stand including the grand larceny charge for the Wingate jewels they'd recovered. The phone conversation she'd recorded was the diamond amongst all the other gems, and Victor didn't stand a chance.

He'd been crazy to think he could play double jeopardy with the Wingate jewels and simply disappear. Fencing fakes for a cool five million and then to turn around and sell the originals for an extra seven million was doubly greedy and doubly dangerous. It was a good thing for Victor he was in prison, because the details of his arrest were no secret. A passport with his picture and a new name and a one-way airline ticket to the Cayman Islands were found in his desk. If he ever managed to get out of prison, Antonio, and whoever had hired him, would hunt him down, looking to extract revenge for his double dealing.

Dakota stood on the back deck enjoying the view. Colt was due home soon, and she couldn't wait to tell him the baby had kicked. The wind blew her hair in her face, and she made a move to capture it and brush it aside.

"Leave it," Colt said huskily, suddenly standing next to her.

"But it's a mess," she said, smiling up at her husband.

"I love it. It goes with the new carefree you."

"Stop." She laughed, punching him lovingly on the arm.

"It's true. Love and motherhood look amazing on you. I'll have to see what I can do to keep you this way."

"You're such a romantic." She couldn't wait another minute to share the wonderful news. "The baby kicked today."

"That's exciting. Will I be able to feel?" Colt looked down at her in amazement.

"Maybe, but only if he's awake and your hands happen to be right here," she said, drawing his arms around her waist.

"Well, then I guess I'll have to make sure I'm holding you all the time. Wouldn't want to miss a single second. Of the baby or you, my darling wife."

If you enjoyed this sweet and charming romance, be sure to check out the
ALSO BY ELSIE DAVIS section on the next page for more clean and wholesome romance.

BONUS READ

Want to keep in touch with new releases and what's happening in the world of Elsie Davis? Sign up for the monthly newsletter at Elsie Davis HEA (Happily-Ever-After) and enjoy DIGGING THE DRIVER (A Celebrity Corgi Romance) as a FREE BOOK!

The greatest compliment you could give an author is to leave a review in order to help other readers discover the same great stories you enjoyed. Amazon/Bookbub/Goodreads are all great places. Many thanks!!!
Another great way to keep in touch - *Follow Elsie Davis on FaceBook*

Also By

Sweet, Clean and Wholesome Stories...with a Happily-Ever-After Guarantee!

Holidays in Hallbrook
(Sweet Romance Series for Holidays Throughout the Year)
Welcome to Hallbrook, New Hampshire. A small-town filled with the unexpected, lots of love, and of course, a beloved dog to ramp up the excitement.
Love & Order (Labor Day)
Love & Family (Thanksgiving)
Love & Peace (Christmas)
Love & Chocolate (Valentine's Day)
Love & Hope (Mother's Day)
Love & Liberty (Independence Day)

Love & Honor (Veteran's Day)
Love & Joy (Easter)
Love & Adventure (Father's Day)

Great Smoky Mountain Getaways
(Christian Inspirational – Women's Fiction Romances)
Juliet's Journey to Love
Poppy's Path to Love
Rachel's Road to Love

Crossroads Creek Cowboys
(Christian Inspirational Romances)
The Heart of a Cowboy
The Help of a Cowboy
The Return of a Cowboy
Coming Soon – The Care of a Cowboy

Crestfield Inn Romances
If you like special kinds of soulmates, a splash of the supernatural, and wholesome relationships, you'll adore this sweet bit of fun filled with romance and mystery.

Turning Back Time
Turning Up Roses
Turning Down Pie

Celebrity Corgi Romance
(Standalone Sweet Romance)
If you like light mystery mixed in with
your happily-ever-after, you'll enjoy this sec-
ond-chance romance and the race to save an
adorable Corgi.
Digging the Driver

Gold Coast Retrievers
(Sweet Romance)
*Special Golden Retrievers help their humans
solve mysteries, save lives, and even find love...*
Defending Dakota

Trinity River
(Sweet Western Romance)
*Ranchers and farmers depend on the Trinity
River for water, but when a secret conglom-
erate starts buying up property by fair means*

or foul, it's time for the landowners of Tumble County to fight back—Texas style. But what they don't count on, is finding love in the process.

Back in the Rancher's Arms

Small Town, Big Secrets

Coming Soon! (2023-2024)

Sundancer's Legacy – 9 Book series

Sundancer's Star

Sundancer's Joy

Sundancer's Heart

Sundancer's Majesty

Sundancer's Miracle

Sundancer's Glory

Sundancer's Kiss

Sundancer's Moon

Sundancer's Splendor

About the Author

Elsie Davis is a *USA Today and International Bestselling Author* of over 25 sweet, clean, and wholesome romances, and a member of the ACFW. She discovered the world of Happily-Ever-After romance at the age of twelve when she began avidly reading Barbara Cartland, the Queen of Romance, and has been hooked ever since. After building her dream log home on top of a small mountain, she turned her attention to do what she loves most, writing. Elsie writes sweet Contemporary Romance and Contemporary Christian Romance from her heart...hoping to share a little love in a big world.

When she's not writing, she can be found birding, kayaking, camping, fishing, playing disc golf, and taking nature walks—hoping to spot wildlife. Basically, she loves all things outdoors, EXCEPT cold weather. She and her husband are avid Caribbean cruisers, but Elsie's favorite vacation was their cruise to Alaska. (In spite of the cold!) Indoors, she enjoys a toasty fire, and of course, a great romance with a guaranteed Happily-Ever-After.

https://www.elsiedavishea.com